# OUTSIDE PEOPLE

## AND OTHER STORIES

Copyright © 2017 Mariam Pirbhai

Except for the use of short passages for review purposes, no part of this book may be reproduced, in part or in whole, or transmitted in any form or by any means, electronically or mechanically, including photocopying, recording, or any information or storage retrieval system, without prior permission in writing from the publisher or a licence from the Canadian Copyright Collective Agency (Access Copyright).

 Canada Council for the Arts / Conseil des Arts du Canada

We gratefully acknowledge the support of the Canada Council for the Arts and the Ontario Arts Council for our publishing program. We also acknowledge the financial support of the Government of Canada.

Cover design: Val Fullard

*Outside People and Other Stories* is a work of fiction. All the characters and situations portrayed in this book are fictitious and any resemblance to persons living or dead is purely coincidental.

Library and Archives Canada Cataloguing in Publication

Pirbhai, Mariam, 1970-, author
    Outside people and other stories / short fiction by Mariam Pirbhai.

(Inanna poetry & fiction series)
Issued in print and electronic formats.
ISBN 978-1-77133-433-4 (softcover).-- ISBN 978-1-77133-434-1 (epub).--
ISBN 978-1-77133-435-8 (Kindle).-- ISBN 978-1-77133-436-5 (pdf)

    I. Title. II. Series: Inanna poetry and fiction series

PS8631.I73O98 2017          C813'.6          C2017-905375-2
                                              C2017-905376-0

Printed and bound in Canada

 MIX Paper from responsible sources FSC® C004071

Inanna Publications and Education Inc.
210 Founders College, York University
4700 Keele Street, Toronto, Ontario M3J 1P3 Canada
Telephone: (416) 736-5356   Fax (416) 736-5765
Email: inanna.publications@inanna.ca  Website: www.inanna.ca

# OUTSIDE PEOPLE

## AND OTHER STORIES

### MARIAM PIRBHAI

inanna poetry & fiction series

INANNA PUBLICATIONS AND EDUCATION INC.
TORONTO, CANADA

*To Ronaldo,
alma de mi alma*

# TABLE OF CONTENTS

Air Raids
1

Chicken Catchers
15

Corazon's Children
31

Toronto's Dominions
48

Sunshine Guarantee
63

Bread and Roti
80

Thirty-Five Seconds
100

Crossing Over
114

Outside People
133

Glossary
144

Acknowledgements
153

*Crumpled scraps of paper adding up to a beautiful life were gathered before me. Amazed, I started feeling its contours.*
　　　　—Ismat Chughtai, "Choti Apa" ("Little Sister")

*One writes against one's solitude and against the solitude of others.*
　　　　—Eduardo Galeano, *Las Venas Abiertas de América Latina (Open Veins of Latin America)*

# AIR RAIDS

*H*E APPROACHED HER *on the* Métro *between McGill and Mont Royal. He said he spent most of his life in the air, instructing people how to save themselves in the event of crash landings. They missed their stops but neither shied away from admitting as much. They knew what it was like to find themselves between stops, and people. Perhaps the sheer impossibility of a prolonged exchange compelled her to ask him to look her up the next time he had the luxury of standing still. It was an honest response, like the smile that dominated her expression at the touch of a warm breeze. He knew what it meant to require the heat to smile. She knew they would meet again, above ground, out in the open.*

\* \* \*

He called as she felt he would.

   She hoped a brisk walk to his hotel in the sunshine would help cast off the cloud hanging over her and, with it, the residual arctic air of an early summer morning. She had read that such bouts of melancholia were a normal part of the grieving process. By the time she reached the next intersection it was clear there was more to it. Today was an anniversary of sorts—the day she and her parents had become naturalized citizens. It should have been one of their better days, but the rawness of her father's nerves had soured the event—or, at least, her recollection of it. How many times had he scrutinized the "notice to appear," or insisted they practice reciting the national anthem, as if citizenship could be denied to those only pretending to sing "O Canada" in the judge's presence. When she asked him why they should swear allegiance to the same Queen their country had rejected, he shot her a disapproving look, saying, "This is your country now."

As she rounded the corner onto boulevard de Maisonneuve, a frigid wind tunnel taunted her overestimation of the sun's power in a northern climate. Even after all these years, she brooded, warmth was the only natural condition she craved, immediately regretting the response as an act of betrayal in a way that only an immigrant's daughter could.

She tried to focus on her destination as she approached the Complexe Desjardins, an imposing edifice with an unobstructed view to the public events held in the expansive plaza at the heart of the Quartier des Spectacles, the city's arts and entertainment district. She walked along its periphery, thinking of the invisible border between the city's eastern and western selves, the clash not of civilizations but of two founding nations still shackled to the trajectory of conquest, when empires fought on the high seas for sugar cane and slaves, or slit each other's throats with bayonets across the Plains of Abraham. Only now the war was waged on different plains, like school curricula, store-front signage, rival public holidays, and legislative bills.

She passed the street-level entrance to the Montreal symphony, just a few metres behind a talkative group setting down placards and banners on the plaza's steps. A curious sight, she thought, since it was too early for the annual jazz festival that would fill the streets with beer tents and concert stages in the weeks to come. And it was too early for any other kind of event, including her own Sunday morning dalliance.

If it weren't for the fact that this was the only time they could meet, before his airline made its return trip to Morocco, she would still be lazing in bed, waking up to the heady odours of roasting coffee beans from the numerous cafés surrounding her apartment in the trendy streets of Plateau Mont Royal. She was one of the lucky ones. She had nabbed her apartment for a steal before the Plateau's gentrification, beating out other applicants because the landlord had taken an immediate liking to her. "You're different. You'll be a good tenant," were his exact words. She wasn't sure if it was her difference or their shared foreignness that put him at ease. It turned out that Mr. Somek was a Sephardic Jew from Iraq who made his fortune when the textile industry was a mainstay of the Montreal economy.

Such revelations might have eluded her had Kostas—Somek's oldest tenant who managed the *dépanneur* on the first floor of her three-storey dwelling—not been a busybody with a fondness for local trivia, an animate version of the tabloids he couldn't keep from flying off his dusty shelves. It was Kostas who told her the life story of Plateau Mont Royal, named for the city and the little mountain that stood at its epicentre. Though it was renowned as the Latin Quarter because of the thriving francophone enclaves of artists, intellectuals, and, increasingly, Beamer-driving yuppies who lived there, this was but a recent incarnation. It had belonged, not so long ago, to the new immigrants and to the workers, as much as any set of streets, parks, schools, shops, and houses could belong to anyone. One community squeezed out the other. Apparently, that was the way it worked around here. No one ever referred to it as a cause-effect relationship, but, like the green-and-white flowers block-printed on her summer dress, the pattern was hard to ignore. "Look at Park Extension!" Kostas lamented, referring to his own working class neighbourhood just north of the Plateau. His family had lived there for three generations. Now, according to Kostas, you couldn't buy a decent souvlaki or find a reliable travel agent on the entire stretch of rue Jean Talon between l'Acadie and avenue du Parc. Since it had morphed from Little Greece to Little India, Kostas said, his family had joined the exodus west and north, into the suburban sprawl at the island-city's limits.

In fact, she had wanted to correct him, his beloved old neighbourhood was not so much a Little India as it was a Little Pakistan, where local businesses bore names like 786 or *Khan Brothers Video and Paan Shop*, given the recent influx of refugees from the country's northern region at the foot of the Himalayan range. Her parents used to describe this sublime part of the country as the "Switzerland of the East," a far cry from the images of U.S. drone attacks, terrorist cells, and cross-border warfare that now dominated the news. And the Little Pakistan that was changing the face of Montreal's western half was only matched by the ever-burgeoning Petit Maghreb in the city's eastern half. Soon enough, the two would meet in the centre, their shared symbols of Arabic calligraphy adorning mosques and community centres, colourful boutiques, specialty grocers, and family-friendly restaurants, fusing together a place so long divided by language and history.

Before she entered the Complexe Desjardins, which apart from a mall, restaurants, and office towers housed the five-star hotel accommodating his airline crew, she deliberated whether she had time enough to smoke a cigarette, a habit she had officially broken, more or less. The rumblings of the gathering crowd drowned out the battle of mind-over-matter raging within her and she threw another glance across the street. This time she could make out some of the wording on the placards.

MULTI-FAITH GATHERING FOR PEACE.

VIVE LE QUÉBEC LIBRE POUR TOUS.

QUÉBEC IS NOT FRANCE.

And the largest one: "I AM NOT A SYMBOL. I AM A PERSON."

The placards were clearly directed at the government's recently proposed legislation to ban religious symbols in the public sector. The controversial bill dubbed the "Charter of Values" had made headlines for weeks, with groups of all religious backgrounds calling it a violation of religious freedoms or an attack on multiculturalism, itself the haloed credo of the nation. Satisfied with her discovery and the momentary diversion it offered, she suppressed any further cravings and pushed open a heavy-set glass door. With her back to the morning light, the reflection of another placard caught her eye, the words CHARTER OF SHAME obliquely burned into her retina like a sunspot. As she made her way through the dimly-lit air-conditioned building, she cursed the paradox of a society that complained about a half-year long winter only to imprison themselves in refrigerators at the first hint of summer. A courtyard fountain, which seemed oddly out of place in the hotel lobby's carpeted interior, provided a welcome refuge, far enough from the prying eyes of bored receptionists, but in plain sight of all the major entrances and exits.

Finding her patiently seated at the fountain's edge, he stooped to kiss her on the lips without a trace of awkwardness, as if theirs was a long-nurtured intimacy. He admired her summer dress, remarking that the first time they had met she was wearing jeans and a white T-shirt—"like a *real* American," he snickered light-heartedly. Then he traced the back of his hand along her bare arm, until his fingers reached the gold pendant resting just above her cleavage. She had been meaning to shorten the chain. The pendant was a childhood gift from her father. She wore it in the same spirit with which she cherished the twelve jingling-jangling gold bangles she had worn religiously since his death. She could swear the bangles had made an impression on her skin, either from the weight of all that precious metal, or from memories weighed down by the alchemy of mourning. On the days she felt resilient and on top of the world, the physical explanation suited her just fine; on most other days, only the metaphysical explanation seemed commensurate with the depths of her grief. Today was an odd sort of day, eliciting neither extreme.

Holding the chain between his fingers, he recited by rote the *surah* engraved on the pendant. She liked the way he made the *ayat al-kursi* rise and fall the way she couldn't. He took possession of the *surah* in the language that brought its inscription—the words she held like an epitaph against her skin—to life. His recitation was redolent with belief, whereas hers was distorted by the utterings of a childhood in rebellion, reminding her of what she was and wasn't, who she was and wasn't, where she was and wasn't. She blushed in embarrassment, checking herself against the invisible judge and jury she carried around like a worn-out lipstick in a purse.

"*Qu'est-ce que tu t'en souviens de notre première rencontre?*" he asked about their first encounter, the nearness of his breath so warm against her skin.

"*Que nous avons oublié nos destinations. Tu as manqué ton arrêt, et moi, le mien,*" she answered back in the language her brain and tongue still struggled to accommodate. "*Et quand tu as vu ce pendentif, tu as pensé que je suis, comme toi, Arabe.*"

He said her eyes had given her origins away: the russet brown of a Medjool date, the variety that his family preferred for *iftar*, when breaking their fast during Ramadan.

"I haven't fasted since we came here," she said, instinctually falling back on English. "But I will never forget the first *iftar* we shared as a family—I mean, as an entire nation, waking, eating, and dreaming in unison, at least for one brief moment."

"*Donc, nous sommes d'une seule famille,*" he declared, gently setting the pendant back down against her skin.

"Yes, tell me more about your family ... about yourself." Was he amused, she couldn't tell, but thought a little curiosity unobtrusively expressed was worth the risk of mockery.

She was a novelty at best, a deviant at worst. For surely he was accustomed to two kinds of women: the ones who helped turn each of his stopovers into an inevitable embrace, the kind who rendered bearable the din of passengers demanding headsets or airline meals, or made the increased suspicion of airport security a surmountable indignity. These were, like his passengers, women of the air, ephemeral, existing in the parentheses of life. And there was the other kind: the woman who would become the mother of his children; the one with whom he would break his fast and observe the various and sundry rituals required of the faithful. The woman he would barely need to speak with because she would complete all his sentences for him, existing as she did on solid ground, in the main clause of life.

Virgin and whore. Redemption and sin. Did he really look at her this way, through the lens of an either/or conditional? Or was this her defence against the possibility that if there was more to him, she would have to adjust the visual syntax of an orientalizing gaze? Or was she looking at him through the prism of her own upbringing, not his? At any rate, here she was: a neither/nor by anyone's and everyone's standards.

"What would you like to know?" he indulged, taking her hand and leading her toward the elevator.

When they got to his room, the curtains were fully drawn, hugging tightly to the illusion of night but not enough to drown out the muffled sounds of the people gathering below. She walked over to the curtained wall, parting the heavy folds to look down at the plaza. From this new perspective, the tops of people's heads, many of which were dressed with hats and other kinds of head coverings, wove in and out of each other in tapestries of colour. Then her eyes rested on the more sobering sight of television news vans, police cars, and the RCMP amassing along street corners, at the ready to shield the crowd against itself.

She felt his arm graze past her shoulder. He closed the curtain, shutting out the little light streaming into the room, as if the sun and the shadows cast on the world below belonged to a time and place that didn't matter, as if she had entered the twilight that seemed to define this virtual stranger's existence. For wasn't he so far away from home—she let her mind wander as he gently coaxed her away from the window—far enough that she could well imagine a mother fretting over the child she had given over to the necessities of survival? For some reason, she imagined him to be the eldest child sacrificed for the sake of the youngest—at least for the one who still carried the ember of a mother's belief in a man's innate right to greatness. How else could a mother endure a job that put her son in harm's way each time he took to the air? At least before the world had started pointing accusatory fingers at airborne Muslims, his job had given him certain liberties as a global citizen. Now, because of this same mobility, he was an object of suspicion at any port of entry and every guarded exit.

She thought of her own parents' anguish when she had insisted they release her to the unknown, where she could live outside the purview of their vigilance. Had they not also succumbed to the unthinkable out of necessity? She had wanted to study painting and art history, but she was an only child, bearing the levity of dreams and the inevitability of sacrifice in equal measure. With a university admittance in hand, she put the distance of a province between them, only to find herself working long hours proofing data for the Québec Ministry of Education's English-language website. It still afforded a kind of freedom, at least until she got locked into the job for the sake of the very same house she dared leave behind, mortgaging her future against a father's compulsion to put down roots on foreign soil, willing her to occupy a state of mind that was, for others, a birthright. But how could she stand by and watch them lose a house when it was their only stake in a land that made them feel like trespassers on its less charitable days, the sort of day that condemned a child of immigrants, no different than herself, to cross the threshold of manhood shackled to a holding cell or an island-prison? She could never have anticipated that in her father's absence, her mother's dreams would be so different, encouraging her to forget the house and attend the university she had travelled all this way for.

And what manner of place is this? she asked herself in his embrace. Was she returning home in the arms of a brother? Or was she stepping into uncharted waters with the baggage of a denizen? Was she the canyon at the foot of his precipice, the slackened grip on all that he held sacred? Did he approve of her *beau corps*, of the way he could address her with open hands, not words, and leave himself protected? Would he approve of her slight reluctance as he unfastened her summer dress? Why did she now hesitate to reveal herself, feeling a naked shoulder blade, an outer thigh, an arched sole were all too much to bare?

She sat up and brushed out the knots in her hair with her fingers, distracting herself from another craving, concealing her self-consciousness. She saw his flight attendant's uniform hanging by the door like the empty shell of someone lost to the constant crossing over of time zones, land, and sea.

"Let's get out of here," she said anxiously.

"Is something wrong?"

"I need some air ... and I could use a cigarette."

"Of course ... *tu fumes trop*."

Was this a judgment or a question? She wasn't sure, and decided not to tell him she had quit, officially. "This used to be a smoker's city. Maybe if I lived somewhere else, I'd smoke less. Or maybe I'd smoke just as much, but try to hide it." And maybe if I lived somewhere else you wouldn't be lying here with me, she wanted to say but didn't.

"*Peut-être*," he smiled vaguely.

As they sipped their coffee in one of those all-day breakfast places, he asked her where she would like to go if she could travel—a stock question she presumed he reserved for the countless mornings spent in hotel lounges with those countless other women of the air. The waitress appeared with his breakfast order, saving her from having to manufacture an equally stock response.

While the waitress made room for an oversized plate, she noted that a part of the order was smothered in bacon bits— the pre-packaged kind that was standard Canadian fare but would no doubt elude the unsuspecting traveller. This time she didn't hesitate, unable to let the observation pass without due comment, wondering if his gratitude was real or fake as he rejected the plate of food before him, wondering if, and for whose benefit, he was laying on the beckoned explanation about *halal* a little thick.

In an effort to ignore the waitress's mounting displeasure, she turned her attention elsewhere, surprised to see how much the crowds outside had grown since the early morning. They flowed out of the plaza and onto the streets, large groups standing not too far from the same wall of glass that had captured the placard's reflection.

"Charter of Shame," she said in a half-whisper.

"*Pardon?*" he asked distractedly.

"*Rien,*" she answered, drawn into the sea of faces that mirrored the message on many of the placards—LA DIVERSITÉ EST UNE RICHESSE. With their constant ebb and flow, however, she saw other kinds of messages: ÉTAT LAÏC, INDIVIDUS LIBRES. QUÉBEC JE ME SOUVIENS.

He asked what she was looking at so intently.

"A stormy Sunday."

"Should I be worried? About my flight?" He swivelled himself around to see what she was seeing, then took her hand and stroked it softly.

"No rings," he observed.

She, too, was being tested. Was she a sister or an impostor? Why wasn't she married?

She pulled her hand away: "No rings. No ties. No worries, right?"

He took out his phone and showed her a picture of himself seated at a festive table laden with several large *tajines*, an array of flatbreads and platters of fruit, his arm around a beautiful young woman, both of them grinning.

"Should *I* be worried?" she stopped herself from blurting out unintentionally.

"Last Eid. Me and my youngest sister," he smiled. "We're very close."

"Ah," she sighed. "She's lovely."

"She doesn't veil herself—*comme tu peux voir*. One of my older sisters wears *hijab*, but the modest kind, like the ones that seem more common here. Maybe that's why they all tease my uncle's wife for spending a fortune on the designer headscarves she sees the actresses wearing in those Egyptian films."

"Tell me more."

"There are many in Morocco who dislike the *niqab*. It's Wahabi, they say."

She looked at him quizzically

"A Saudi custom," he clarified. "An import. Some go so far as to support the French in their ban, and others say that even focusing on these issues is a waste of time, or worse: a kind of subterfuge—just another attack on Islam by the West."

The waitress reappeared. "Bacon-free, as you order," she said peevishly in English, in spite of the fact that he had only spoken to her in French, a language he clearly possessed with native fluency. She waited for his reaction, secretly hoping he wouldn't let the waitress get away with it. She knew how it felt to make every effort to speak French in a place that insisted on it, only to be answered back in English. She had always chalked it up to her accent, her grammar, her slowness in another language. Now she wasn't so sure.

He seemed too tired to notice or care. He barely glanced at the plate before pushing it toward the middle of the table: "Eat with me."

"I'm not hungry."

"You'll be hungry when you start eating."

She yielded.

"Next time I'll be here for two days," he said.

"Next time?"

"We could meet at your place? *Oui?*"

"Then you should know where to find me," she said, surprised by the turn their morning had taken. She wrote down her address on a paper napkin and then found herself writing her name in Urdu, the mother tongue she had only recently recovered from oblivion, like a child learning the alphabet for the first time. He scrutinized her Urdu script in affectionate amusement. To him it must have looked like misspelled Arabic.

"*Alors, c'est possible de me retrouver ... aussi,*" he said, describing his hometown just north of Marrakesh.

When she mentioned it was time to go, he insisted on walking out with her. A concentrated shock of light hit their eyes as soon as they left the building. The light turned out to be part of a camera man's recording equipment. It was directed at a young woman wearing a pair of jeans, a pink *hijab*, and a long-sleeved T-shirt with the printed words KEEP CALM AND WEAR HIJAB, a slogan that matched the self-assuredness with which she was speaking to the reporter. Something about the scene reminded her of a photograph of her mother when she was younger. She was standing on a beach in *shalwar kameez*, her long brown hair blowing freely in the coastal winds whipped up by the Arabian Sea. It was the kind of photo that children look at askance, seeing a version of a parent's younger self they barely recognize. But now she vividly recalled her mother's expression, so wide-eyed and confident, and utterly unfazed by the blazing sunlight refracted against a crowded Karachi shoreline. Not just an image of things she barely recognized, but of a person she longed to know.

"*Why did you feel it was important to participate in today's demonstration?*" she heard the reporter ask.

She moved in closer, eager to hear the young woman's response.

"*I was born here,*" she replied. "*And yet I'm being told that because of what I wear on my head, I'm a threat to this society. But isn't this my society too? Am I a threat to myself?*"

"*But the proposed Charter of Values is directed at all religious symbols, not just your own,*" the reporter persisted.

"*That is why we're here as a multi-faith march, in solidarity with those from other religions, including our Christian brothers and sisters.*"

"*Yet many in the Muslim community say this proposal only came about because the first one, the Reasonable Accommodation bill directed specifically at Muslims, was rejected. What do you think about this?*"

"*Well, the fact of the matter is that both then and now we marched in solidarity with people of all faiths and beliefs, from the religious and secular communities.*"

"*How do you think this bill will affect you personally, in your everyday life?*"

"*I'm already affected because I'm worried about my future. I want to study Public Administration, but now I feel this will not be a good choice for me, since this bill will make it impossible for me to work in the government or the public sector. My career and job prospects will be compromised. My degree will be worthless...*"

"All the streets are closed," he shouted over to her from the corner where he had stationed himself, scrutinizing the police blockades. She nodded, trying to catch the rest of the interview, but the reporter had quickly moved onto someone else, the young woman and her pink *hijab* having melded seamlessly back into the crowd.

"We can walk another block to the *Métro*, if you wish," he said.

"Don't worry. I'll get back home the way I came."

"Through this?"

"I'll manage. You just have a safe flight tonight," she said, kissing him on the cheek.

"A safe flight, yes. A safe flight," he repeated the phrase like a chant she had set in motion, just as he had read the *surah* on her pendant, resurrecting it in ways that made it pulsate against her skin.

He kissed her hand, and she looked at the people spilling out into the streets in and around the Quartier des Spectacles.

In another second she was pulled into the crowd, brushing up against a tall woman with wiry dreadlocks poking out of a

Rastafarian hat. The woman held up a placard with the words ONE LOVE, ONE HEART scrolled onto it in green, black, and yellow. A group of older men and women in front of her carried a banner saying, MY RIGHT, MY LIFE, MY CHOICE, and two teenage girls waved a makeshift placard that read: HOODIES AND HIJABS 4 SOCIAL JUSTICE. She heard the woman with the Rastafarian hat make some comment to her friend about the glorious sunshine as she peeled off her cardigan and tied it round her waist.

"*My Right!*" people chanted in unison, while making their way down rue Ste-Catherine, the city's main commercial street that ran from east to west.

She threw a glance back over an array of bobbing heads and placards but he was long out of view.

"...*My Life!*" the chanting continued.

She gave up on the idea of going back home the way she came, releasing herself to the current.

"*My Choice!*" she joined in, certain they would meet again, on solid ground. Out in the open.

# CHICKEN CATCHERS

*In memory of the ten migrant workers who lost their lives on February 6, 2012, near Stratford, Ontario, in one of the worst road accidents in Ontario's history. And for the three men who survived.*

"THE VAN LEAVING!" Hector bellowed from the doorway of the bunkhouse that housed him and twelve other men.
Reggie gently prodded the man lying on the cot next to his. "Amaru, wake up!" Amaru grunted and weakly pulled the steel-grey blanket over his ears.
"*Ándale, amigo!*" Hector held the door open with one gloved hand, fumbling to pull on the second glove with his teeth. Reggie wanted to caution Hector not to bite down on the same gloves he wore while handling the chickens, certain they were contaminated. Then he thought better of it. Hector saw himself as a mentor to the other men. In all fairness, he helped Reggie buy gloves when it was abundantly clear that no one would be supplying him protective gear for their work on the poultry farms. The gloves had eaten into the little money he had set aside for a winter coat, but Hector assured him an affordable coat could be found when the time came. The gloves, on the other hand, were indispensable.
"You must find a pair thin enough to grab a chicken by the neck, and thick enough to save your own neck!" Hector laughed, pleased with his joke, more so because he had made

it in English, which he spent the evenings teaching himself on one of those language-learning programs.

*Grab one chicken by the neck?* Reggie had balked. That hardly seemed worth the price of the gloves!

"No, no no!" Hector chided. "*No solamente un pollo por mano, hermanito! Cuatro pollos por mano!*"

Reggie looked perplexed, so Hector translated: "One chicken, one hand—no good! Lose job. *Hasta luego!* Four chickens, one hand. Eight chickens, two hands. First you catch, then you hold." Hector splayed out his fingers in demonstration: "Hold neck between fingers. Like this. Five fingers, four necks. *Comprendes?*"

Reggie still couldn't hold more than three chickens in one hand, but he was faster at catching them than anyone else. By day's end he managed to round up as many chickens as the other men.

"*Vámanos!*" Hector urged again.

Reggie caught a glimpse of the white van that transported them to the poultry barns, its headlights illuminating a "Danger: Keep Out" sign on a massive shed containing the farm's overstock of pesticides.

"Amaru!" Reggie placed his hand on the sleeping man's hunched shoulders and felt him shivering under the blankets.

"Hector! Amaru's sick!"

"*Sí!*" Hector countered. "Sick on tequila, maybe!"

"He's sick, I tell you!"

"Why he is your problem?" Hector was growing increasingly impatient. Their wages would be deducted if the driver was delayed.

Reggie hesitated. Then he heard Amaru mutter something under his breath. He leaned in, resisting the temptation to run his hands through Amaru's generous crop of black, glossy hair.

"You say something, man?"

"Hector ... right," an enfeebled voice responded. "Not your problem. Go!"

Reggie smarted at the dismissal. He was about to shout back to Hector to wait up for him when Amaru fell into a coughing spasm that came from somewhere deep within his lungs.

"He's in bad shape. Someone's got to stay," Reggie determined, taking his blanket from his bed and throwing it over Amaru.

As the door swung shut, Reggie could have sworn he heard Hector curse him with the kind of taunts that people hurled at him back home. Like the vitriolic sports commentary broadcast in the aftermath of any defeat suffered by the West Indies cricket team—an unforgiveable sin in the eyes of his countrymen—Reggie had heard every possible brand of derisive speculation about "his type."

Reggie relaxed when he heard the driver rev up the van. As the wheels crunched down on the dirt road running through the Dumfrey family's three-hundred acre farm, he vowed not to dwell on Hector and the other men, several of whom had arrived only a week ago, and whose names he didn't even know.

Seeing that Amaru had quieted down, Reggie stretched out on his cot, grateful for the chance to close his eyes. Within minutes he drifted off to sleep.

A dog barking somewhere in the distance jolted Reggie awake, his heart skipping a beat in thinking he had missed the van and an entire day's pay.

"Él ... es," Reggie heard Amaru mumble.

"Amaru?" Reggie whispered, not wanting to startle him.

"Élesa...."

A woman's name aroused a pang of jealousy, but this didn't stop Reggie from springing into action. He had purchased some over-the-counter medicines on one of their brief Sunday shopping trips—stuff that the pharmacist recommended to fight off what he called the local range of common afflictions. Assessing Amaru's symptoms, Reggie rooted through a shoebox containing a packet of antihistamines, an ointment for muscle and joint pain relief, nasal spray, eye drops, Extra Strength Cold and Flu medication, and a bottle of aspirin.

"Amaru, you must take some medicine," Reggie touched the man's shoulder softly. Amaru acknowledged Reggie through half closed eyes, managing to take a sip of water from the bottle long enough to wash down a pill. Expending all of his energy on this one small act, Amaru fell back onto his pillow and was lost to a bout of fitful sleep.

Reggie sat vigil this time, partly to watch for signs of further distress and partly to seize the opportunity to study, in unhindered admiration, his new-found patient. Amaru was not handsome in any way that Reggie was familiar with. As a Jamaican whose own family was as "mix-up as *callaloo*," as his grandmother liked to say, Reggie thought he had seen every gradation of skin colour and every type of face created under the heavens. But Amaru was as foreign an ingredient as any he had encountered. It was a combination of things: Amaru's brown skin held undertones of the deepest reds, like the earth below an Amazonian river or at the inner core of a setting sun. Amaru's kind, intelligent eyes were as black as the heart of a dormant volcano. They sat below a wide forehead and above cheekbones that seemed unusually pronounced for a man, even in Reggie's estimation. The overall effect was alluring, particularly when Amaru laughed and revealed deep-set creases that wizened his otherwise youthful face.

"Élesa ... *espe* ... *ra* ... *me*," Amaru sputtered.

Reggie leaned in closer just as Amaru shifted to his right side. The movement launched another coughing spasm and forced Amaru to lift himself onto his elbows. Opening his eyes a little more than he had the first time, he looked up at Reggie. "You stay? Why?"

Reggie winced, feeling thwarted again. He reached for the water bottle and handed it to Amaru. "You can't see you're really sick, man. Shivering and shaking like the leaves out there."

"I no sick. I work," Amaru feebly threw off the blankets and hauled himself into a seated position. Before Reggie had a chance to object, Amaru fell back into the cot.

"*Cha!*" Reggie exclaimed, re-covering Amaru with the blankets. Seeing Amaru yield to his ministrations, Reggie furtively touched Amaru's temple. It was burning up.

Reggie thought he should try to assess the seriousness of Amaru's condition, launching what he imagined to be a series of "doctorly" questions: How long have you had that cough: More than one week? *Sí.* More than two? *Sí.* More than a month? *Sí.* Have you had any other symptoms, like nausea, vomiting ... bleeding? *Sí* and *sí* to the first and second, Amaru nodded, but *no* to the third. Reggie breathed a sigh of relief. Have you noticed any other symptoms over the past few months, like dizziness, chest pain, headaches, fatigue? Amaru nodded in the affirmative to most of the items on Reggie's list, but indicated that he didn't understand the word "fatigue." Reggie tried to translate in the little Spanish he had picked up from a Dominican lover who had used Jamaica as a clandestine stopover on his migration north. "*Muy can...*" he struggled to recall the word, "*cansado.*"

"*Sí, todo el tiempo.*"

Reggie frowned, unsettled by Amaru's responses. Then Amaru pulled his arms out from under the covers and proceeded to scratch his forearm. "*Y cómo se dice...*"

"Itchy?"

"*Sí, sí*, itchy," Amaru nodded, and placed his arms under the covers again.

Reggie was hoping Amaru had a case of the flu, which would run its course. But these were chronic symptoms, a few of which Reggie, himself, was starting to experience, like itchy skin and the occasional dizzy spell. It was clear Amaru required medical attention but Reggie was at a loss. He had no choice but to wait for the driver and Hector. They would know who to call or at least how far the nearest hospital was.

Without the boisterous chatter of the other men filling up the bunkhouse, Reggie realized how isolated they were, and how little he knew of his surroundings. They were picked up so early in the morning that it was dark out. There was barely a soul on the roads except the occasional freight truck transporting goods—livestock, farming equipment, and the like—to and from the farms. Now that winter had arrived, it was also dark on their drive back to the farm, a loss of daylight hours he felt he could never get used to.

Reggie regretted not taking the time to explore the area while the weather held out. He just could not pull himself out of bed in those early weeks unless he absolutely had to, their long shifts made all the longer because there was nowhere to take a decent break on the farm, most of them stealing a few minutes to relieve themselves behind the poultry barn, or release their hands from their gloves just long enough to eat a sandwich or smoke a cigarette on days that seemed far too cold for such a robust display of vegetation.

Reggie looked over at Amaru who was nodding off again, the bunkhouse eerily quiet except for the sound of an increasingly fierce wind whipping against the flimsy exterior walls. He figured he should be grateful for this rare moment of quiet stillness, but he could not shake the feeling of unease and foreboding brought on by his confinement.

Four months to go, he thought anxiously, counting down his ten-month contract. At least it's going fast, he reassured himself, assessing the time he had already spent here, from the moment of his arrival in the summer. He distinctly recalled being picked up from Pearson International Airport in the same white van, but the driver was not the young man who drove them around locally. He was a much older Latin American man. Apart from a few words of welcome, they shared a silent drive for over an hour before stopping at a city that made him think of his father's old records by the famous calypsonian, Lord Kitchener. After filling up the van with a group of Mexican men, and two or three women, the van exited onto a smaller highway, which opened up to an expanse of rolling hills, endless cornfields, and the kind of pine trees he had only seen in those feel-good

Christmas Hollywood movies. The combination of the scenery and jetlag must have lulled him to sleep. By the time the van entered the Dumfrey estate, he had missed the names of the towns along the way. Nor did he have the chance to talk to his fellow passengers since he was the only one to get off here—the others were on their way to a tobacco farm farther west. This confirmed the recruiter's brief indication that most of the seasonal agricultural work would be needed in the southwestern part of the province, a geography that made little sense to him. Thinking back on all that now, he also recalled some bureaucrat in the Kingston recruitment office making a crack about the workers becoming regular "arts patrons" at some Shakespearean theatre festival the region was famous for. Perhaps in his effort to tune out the clearly intended sarcasm, Reggie had dismissed the comment at the time.

Sure enough, Reggie had seen several posters advertising *King Lear*, one of the few plays he'd enjoyed reading in school, plastered around the stores where the driver took them for a few extra dollars per passenger, so they could buy more supplies. Reggie found the elegant posters so incongruous with the bland one-storey building that housed the stores. As underwhelming as it was, the building contained the basic necessities of any small town: a pharmacy, a coffee shop that was usually packed with crusty old-timers and the stray teenager, the hardware store where they purchased their gloves and boots, and a small bank that the men spent most of their time in, wiring money transfers to family back home. When the driver was less rushed, he would take them to another small strip-mall a few minutes away, where they could buy a bucket of chicken at a KFC, and some beer at a liquor store that, Reggie noted, carried a few bottles of outlandishly over-priced Jamaican rum. Reggie figured that the plaza was a good twenty-minute drive from the farm, which ruled out the possibility of his setting out on his own for help. Some of the men still biked all the way to the stores and even as far as the neighbouring towns, but Reggie could hardly picture himself, a child of the tropics, getting around on a bike in this kind of weather.

At least if they had the facilities, he thought, he could have drawn a hot bath infused with fever grass and cascarilla, one of his grandmother's special cure-alls that would be sure to help break Amaru's fever. But they only had a set of portable toilets at the side of the bunkhouse, which was getting progressively harder to use in the cold. Inside the building there was barely enough space for their beds, a set of lockers, a few dilapidated arm chairs, a small table and four plastic chairs, and a curtained-off area that served as a makeshift kitchen, with a hot plate, a sink, and a relic of a fridge that needed a frequent kick to keep its motor running. Reggie tried to minimize his time in this area because it also contained a single stand-up shower that made the room perpetually damp and mouldy. Only two men per night were permitted to use it and, even then, they agreed not to keep the water running since clean water, much less hot water, was a commodity that came in dribs and drabs.

Holed up in the bunkhouse with no one to talk to, Reggie felt the wretchedness of his predicament get the better of him for the first time in months. He never counted on feeling this bizarre concoction of homesickness and dread, as if the idea of home had taken on the spectre of both ailment and remedy.

Unable to get back to sleep he decided to make himself and Amaru one of his favourite Jamaican brands of herbal tea. It was always a staple in his mother's kitchen, used to help alleviate all manner of stomachaches, including the kind induced by an entire summer spent devouring Julie mangoes. He smiled at the image of his grandmother seeing fit to reprimand the children for their gluttony, and to curse the adults for throwing good money after the commercially packaged teas that had taken over household pantries.

Amaru's eyes were shut when Reggie returned with the tea, so he set the mug down on the stack of crates they used as bedside tables. He was about to prod his sleeping patient awake when

Amaru opened his eyes and thrust his hand forward aggressively. Before Reggie could straighten up, Amaru grabbed Reggie's shirt and pulled him down. "Why you here?" he demanded gruffly, his coiled fist bearing into Reggie's chest.

"*Me cyaan lef yuh deh*," Reggie gasped, lapsing into the Jamaican Creole the recruiter had advised him not to speak in Canada where, he had added for effect, *they only speak the Queen's English*, though Reggie hadn't spoken to enough locals to confirm if this were true.

Amaru's grip tightened, sending a current of heat through Reggie's chest. "*Digame*!"

"I don't understand!" Reggie pleaded. "For ... *dinero*. Like you! Just like you."

Amaru released Reggie with a force that made him stumble. Shaken and disoriented, he managed to set himself down on his cot, his gaze finally resting upon a single set of windows placed at an elevation that no one could see out of, except from a distance. Snow was sticking to the edge of the glass. It wasn't snowing when the men left this morning, he thought vacantly.

"*Discúlpame*," Amaru said contritely, and reached for the tea.

An awkward silence ensued till Reggie ventured, "My father had a farm. A dairy farm."

"A farm? Why you leave?"

"Where to start?" Reggie said, still looking up at the window. "The farm supplied milk. All local. All steady. Till the market got flooded with imported powdered milk. Even mothers were convinced their blesséd milk wasn't good enough for their babies, much less my father's milk. Soon the dairy farm turned into a meat farm, but who's crazy enough to buy one Jamaican cow for the same price as three Guatemalan cows, or two Texan cows, for that matter."

Reggie took a deep breath. "I wanted to study medicine. Not this kind," he said, pointing to his shoebox of pharmaceuticals. "The kind my grandmother knew. But I was eighteen when my father lost the farm, and I ended up in the city looking for work. Factory work sewing Nike shorts. Cleaning rooms at some luxury resort. Pumping gasoline. Selling souvenirs to tourists. I did whatever came my way. But it wasn't easy. I got turned away more than I got hired." Then, more to himself than to Amaru, he said: "I'm bad for business, *naah mean*."

Reggie snuck a sideways glance at Amaru. "Then I met this guy who was just getting back from seasonal work up North, picking grapes for some vineyards next to Niagara Falls. He warned me not to go, saying it was like the old days on the *bakra* plantation—*a new kind of slavery*," he clarified. "I thought he was exaggerating. And I hated the city. The idea of getting back to a farm didn't seem so bad. The recruiters only look for *real men*, he said. I'd be crazy to think they'd take me! Maybe there was some truth to what he was saying, but I lucked out. For one, the recruiter needed to fill his seasonal quota and, you know what they say: *nuh jus one way fi heng dog*." Reggie wasn't sure how to translate this. "Let's just say I found a way to give him a little extra incentive. I'm not proud of it...." Reggie bit down on his lower lip, wondering if he'd revealed too much. Deciding it was too late to hold back now, he continued: "The rest was surprisingly easy. He took care of all the paper work. And I just signed on the dotted line: Reggie Taylor.... I was named after my maternal grandmother, you know. Reggie, short for Regina Abigail Taylor, as if my ... well, mothers always know."

"Regina," Amaru repeated, reminded of an article in the *Canadian Geographic* magazines he had purchased at the local thrift shop. "*Como la ciudad*."

"I guess so," Reggie said uneasily. "But you won't mention any of this—to Hector and the other guys, I mean?"

"You is Reggie. Only Reggie."

Reggie and Amaru sat in silence again.

"Your father's farm," Amaru's voice broke the tension. "It have normal cows? And normal chickens?"

Reggie wasn't sure what he was getting at.

"Not like here! *Aqui, muy extraños,*" Amaru grinned broadly. "Strange chickens. Maybe strange cows also!"

"No, not like here! Not like here at all!" Reggie said, relieved to see that Amaru had eased up and that some colour had returned to his face. He reflected on Amaru's observation about the local livestock. He had never thought of it before, but the chickens they had to vaccinate were a little odd. Their breasts were two or three times the size of any chicken he had seen back home. They were so large that the poor creatures wobbled about unsteadily under the weight of their disproportion.

Yet the Dumfrey farm, Reggie had gleaned from Hector, was considered a producer of organic eggs, because the chickens were what they called "free-run." They were free to run all right, but only to make our lives a living hell, Reggie thought resentfully. Day in and day out, all they did was chase after these hapless animals through the din of their clucking and cackling; the heavy thud and steamrolling of their boots cushioned by a slimy cocktail of feces and feathers. And the smell—the unshakeable, putrid smell coming from barns so big they looked like a hundred poultry farms collapsed into one. It was no wonder the workers were hired to ensure every one of those chickens was vaccinated before being put to the slaughter. That was all they were hired to do. Catch the chickens and hold onto them by their necks just long enough for some guy to inject them with antibiotics or some cocktail of drugs, with dosages strong enough to turn even the most unyielding creature into a sad, lifeless lump of flesh. And they had to work so fast that, on more than one occasion, he was quite certain the needle had missed a chicken and pierced through his gloves.

"These chickens don't look right, man!" Reggie laughed.

"Exactly! Why these chicken breast so big?" Amaru laughed back. "In Peru, no one want that part. Everyone want this part!" he added, mustering the energy to slap his leg.

The mention of Peru took Reggie by surprise. He assumed

all the guys were Mexican, like Hector.

"How you say this part, in English?" Amaru asked, pointing to his leg again.

"The thigh," Reggie said. "When we were kids we used to fight over the legs and thighs! My parents even took the white meat so we could get the dark meat!"

"*Lo más sabroso!*"

"Amen!" Reggie concurred. "But everyone want white meat here. Did you see the two-dollar special at *KFC* the last time we were there? A whole meal, with all the sides, but only if you take the thighs!"

"*Sí*! *Muy especial*!"

"Here, dark meat sells cheap."

"Lucky for us!" Amaru said, and the two of them howled with laughter till Amaru's coughing cut their amusement short. He sat up, convulsing with pain, and covered his mouth with his sleeve.

Reggie wasn't sure what to do. He grabbed a face towel from a bag of bathroom supplies stashed under his bed. It was streaked with blood when Amaru handed it back, but Reggie pretended not to notice, not wanting to add to Amaru's distress. He anxiously checked his watch and noted it was barely noon. It would be hours before Hector and the other men returned, hours before they could convince the driver to take Amaru to the nearest hospital. In the effort to do something useful, he placed an extra pillow on Amaru's cot, and motioned for him to lie back once the coughing had subsided. "You need more water, *bredda*? More tea?"

Amaru waved his suggestions away but yielded to Reggie's gentle prodding to lie back.

"I have daughter," Amaru said breathlessly, after settling back on the pillows. "Her name is Élesa." He withdrew a crumpled photo from his shirt pocket and passed it over to Reggie.

"She's beautiful. Like her father," Reggie observed, emboldened by their newfound camaraderie.

"Like her mother," Amaru smiled, the lines deepening around his eyes.

Reggie didn't flinch over the mention of a woman this time. If anything, it comforted him to know that Amaru had a family, that he wasn't alone.

"*Mi hija*: she sick," Amaru continued gravely. "Every month, I send money. For treatment."

"What's wrong with her?"

"Leukemia."

"I'm sorry, man."

"Now I sick. Maybe go to hospital, yes?"

"Yes, as soon as Hector gets back, I'll…"

"No!" Amaru cut him off. "I no have money for hospital here, and for Élesa, there."

"Are you sure you have to pay?" he asked helplessly. He was so grateful to have been recruited, that he had barely looked over the terms of the contract.

"I no have health card. I no take risk."

"That's simple then! We get a card!"

"How?"

Reggie vaguely recalled the recruiter saying something about a probation period after which certain benefits would take effect, but the information had come at him too fast.

"I'll get my contract. Maybe there'll be some information there—a number I can call," Reggie offered, with a renewed sense of purpose. Surely it would be easy enough to make a few phone calls to the Agency or some kind of local representative. After all, what excuse did he have? At least language wasn't a barrier for him—not in the same way it was for Amaru and Hector, or the other men who came here speaking only a few words of English.

"No, all that take time," Amaru objected more forcefully. "If I go now, I pay. Or maybe *el patrón*—the Boss—maybe he have to pay for me. I cannot risk. I need job."

Reggie walked over to a set of lockers, and fished out an

envelope filled with his savings, the equivalent of approximately one month's pay. Unlike the other men, there was no one at home waiting on his remittances. His mother had passed away shortly after they lost the farm, and his father was far too proud to accept any help, at least not Reggie's. If anything, he had always seen Reggie as a liability. The idea of home needled him again, this time enough to consider sticking out this chicken catcher gig for another year, as wretched as it was. In hindsight, no one really bothered him here. Hector and the other guys seemed too preoccupied or too tired to pay him too much mind. It was a new sensation—the space to consider what more one could be when released from the grip of derision. Hadn't his grandmother always said this was his special gift—*to be more than one thing at once*?

Amaru's palpable suffering shored up Reggie's resolve.

"Whatever you need. Just take it! Pay me back whenever," he said, thrusting the envelope into Amaru's hands.

"*No puedo!*" Amaru pushed it back.

"Please! *Por favor!*"

Amaru didn't have the chance to respond, because the door was thrown open by a woman wearing hefty boots and a dusty red jacket that reminded Reggie of the pointed crown of flesh on the chickens' heads. She was carrying a large empty duffle bag, which she set down for time enough to pull down her hood and reveal a messy ponytail. Reggie assumed she was here to check on Amaru, that Hector must have requested a doctor after all. But she didn't as much as look at them. She headed straight for the lockers and set about prying each one open by force with a crowbar.

"Hey, what are you doing?" Reggie protested, rushing over to slam his locker shut. "You can't do that!"

It took the woman a few seconds to register the fact that she was being spoken to, that there were two other people in the room. She said nothing and hurriedly returned to whatever mission she had come to fulfil.

Reggie protested again, making a point of standing sentinel in front of the lockers, his arms crossed defiantly.

"Step aside!" the woman growled, without looking up.

"That's not your property, lady!" Reggie barked back.

"This *is* my property. *All* of this is my property!"

Alarmed by her razor-sharp authority, Reggie stepped aside but remained close. "What happened? Why are you taking their things? Did something happen?"

The woman remained undeterred till every item had been cleared out of the remaining lockers. Then she headed over to the cots, where she proceeded to gather all the men's personal effects, including watches, notebooks, Bibles, even Hector's language CDs—whatever she could find of the men's belongings. She worked at a furious pace before heading for the door.

"Wait! There's a sick man here! He's coughing blood, for god's sake. He needs a doctor!" Reggie ran after her like a storm chaser following the path of an angry tornado.

The woman stopped and turned around, dropping the duffle bag by her feet and using the weight of her back to hold the door open. Wafts of snow and a wicked wind blew into the bunkhouse, dousing the little heat generated over the course of the night.

"What's your name?" the woman asked sternly. Reggie could see that she was much older than she had at first appeared. He also noticed the Dumfrey farm crest on her jacket's upper right breast pocket.

"Regina," he blurted out. "I mean, Reggie. Reggie Taylor."

"And him?" She glanced over at Amaru who was now sitting upright at the edge of his cot, the strain of getting up visible in every line of his angular face.

"Amaru … López," he managed to say, trying to stave off the mounting pressure in his lungs. "Where is Hector? Why you take their things?"

The woman looked at her watch, clearly nervous about

something. "There was an accident this morning. A truck hit the van."

"This morning?" Reggie's mind struggled to catch up: *accident, hit, van.*

"Worst crash of its kind around here. Only one survivor." Then, looking at Amaru, she declared: "You sure picked the right day to be sick, pal. I'd say you're pretty damn lucky."

"Lucky," Amaru repeated, the word floating past Reggie in a cold-induced stream of ghostly vapour.

The woman lifted the duffle bag now heavy with the men's belongings and walked into the blizzard, releasing the door to close on its own. The door started to swing itself shut but couldn't surmount the force of the wind that held it ajar.

"Wait!" Reggie shouted, rushing to the door. "You said 'survivor'? One survivor!"

Reggie's voice was clipped by the sound of the door slamming hard against the bank of snow amassing at the threshold of the bunkhouse.

# CORAZON'S CHILDREN

CORAZON LIGHTLY BRUSHED her feather duster along the outer edges of the framed photographs. Unlike most of the residences she cleaned, there were very few photos cluttering the Hartmans' home. This made her pay more attention to the six black-and-whites they had taken the trouble of having professionally matted and mounted in brushed-silver frames.

In the first frame closest to the front door was a picture of Mr. and Mrs. Hartman. Mrs. Hartman's right hand was interlocked in Mr. Hartman's left hand and pressed close against his chest. Mr. Hartman was an athletic man with a slightly dishevelled crop of greying hair, a strong jaw-line and kind, smiling eyes. Mrs. Hartman looked a lot like the elderly Japanese woman in the portrait displayed among a modest cluster of table-top frames in the living room, the only other set of photos Corazon had come across. She had spotted the resemblance the first time she picked up the photo, surprised by the weight of such a tiny frame. The woman in the photo had Mrs. Hartman's high forehead and the same little gap between her front teeth.

Lucky features, Corazon reflected, turning her attention to the delicate task of cleaning the glass protecting the picture of Mr. and Mrs. Hartman. Corazon admired Mrs. Hartman's tailored ivory suit, cinched at the waist by a belt made of the same silky material. Mr. Hartman was formally dressed too. He was wearing a dark suit and white shirt, though his tie looked just a little bit crooked. Corazon wondered how someone as fastidious as Mrs. Hartman hadn't straightened it out before the picture was taken. Especially when she learned that this was their wedding photo. A Justice of the Peace wedding, Mrs. Hartman had said matter-of-factly on Corazon's first tour around the home, adding: "In fact, my name is Murakami-Hartman—Dr. Murakami-Hartman—but you can call me Janet." Corazon had never referred to a boss by a first name and she had trouble pronouncing "Murakami," so Mrs. Hartman just stuck.

The second photo was of Mr. and Mrs. Hartman rising above an alien landscape in a hot air balloon. "Our honeymoon in Turkey," Mrs. Hartman explained. "In a place called Cappadocia. Which means fairy chimneys because of those funny-looking rocks the region is famous for. People actually live in them you know," she said, pointing out the windows and doorways carved out of one of the larger rocks. An odd place for a honeymoon, Corazon had thought at the time, though now she had grown accustomed to the image, its strangeness neutralized by multiple viewings.

The third photo was of a younger Mrs. Hartman in a long black gown and square hat. "The day I became a doctor—a psychiatrist," she beamed. The fourth photo was of Mr. Hartman at a ribbon-cutting ceremony. He was at the foot of a very long bridge. There were a lot of official looking people standing next to him, all of them grinning artificially for the camera. The people looked familiar and so did the tropical vegetation behind him. "Mr. Hartman's an engineer. That's him at the opening of a new bridge he helped build overseas," Mrs. Hartman explained proudly. It looked a lot like the Philippines, Corazon thought but didn't have a chance to say so because Mrs. Hartman had already moved on to the fifth photo. It was of her this time, hugging two smiling children, a girl and a boy. Corazon thought they looked like her cousin Delia's children, in Los Angeles. "My niece and nephew—my brother's," Mrs. Hartman clarified. And the last photo was of Mr. and Mrs. Hartman again. This one was taken in their home. Corazon recognized the wall of windows overlooking the Vancouver harbour. The only difference was the living room colour: the walls used to be white and now they were painted an elephant grey. Mr. and Mrs. Hartman were sitting in front of a cake with icing script that simply said "Happy 10th." "Our wedding anniversary," Mrs Hartman said. "Taken just a few weeks before the Agency sent you to us."

Corazon noticed the third photo from the right had become a little lopsided, like Mr. Hartman's tie. She walked over to it and straightened it out. It was the one of Mrs. Hartman on her graduation day. She looked a lot like she did in her wedding photo. Understated in her elegance, a pearl choker and a silver wristwatch her only adornment, and the hem of another pencil skirt just peeping through her voluminous black gown. She was shaking the hands of an older man with spectacles. He was handing her a piece of paper rolled into a cylinder. Mrs. Hartman looked so confident, like she could talk to anyone about anything. Corazon could only hope that her daughter Amanda would grow up to be so self-assured. Like Mrs. Hartman.

Corazon stepped back to examine the photos. Mrs. Hartman was very particular. She would notice even the slightest displacement. It wasn't always easy for Corazon to remember exactly at which angle or on what table an object was placed, so she tried her best to clean around the bric-a-brac as much possible. At least the photos hanging in the foyer were easy to manage. They either lined up or they didn't. The second last photo of Mrs. Hartman and her brother's children was definitely off a few degrees, Corazon thought, second-guessing herself. She walked over to reposition it, straining to line it up perfectly with the other five. She examined the picture again as she held the sides of the frame between her hands, nudging it a millimeter this way, then a millimeter that way. The boy was standing behind Mrs. Hartman who was sitting cross-legged on a sloping rock, a waterfall cascading behind them. The boy had his arms wrapped around her neck from behind, and a little girl of no more than three years was sitting in the crook of Mrs. Hartman's crossed legs. Such nice-looking children, Corazon remarked. And Mrs. Hartman looks so happy in their company. It's a wonder she doesn't have any children of her own.

Corazon knew little about the Hartmans. They were never home on the Mondays and alternating Fridays she came to clean. During the first few weeks the Agency assigned her to them, Mrs. Hartman made a point of keeping a watchful eye on Corazon, though she spent most of her time looking over some kind of graph, which Corazon had spotted in the recycling bin on her next visit. It turned out to be a series of graphs, each one corresponding to a single month. When Corazon examined the graph patterns penned in red by, she assumed, Mrs. Hartman, they each looked quite different and Corazon deduced they had something to do with Mrs. Hartman's patients.

Much to Corazon's relief, Mrs. Hartman's vigilance was short-lived. After those first few weeks, Mrs. Hartman must have concluded that Corazon could be trusted, and Corazon let herself in and out of the house, having little contact with Mrs. Hartman, and even less with Mr. Hartman. Until a few months ago, when Mrs. Hartman came home early. She barely said hello, headed to the master bedroom and closed the door behind her with a rather haunting finality. Corazon hadn't cleaned the bedroom yet, and wasn't sure what to do. She was kept to a strict timetable, and even stricter instructions to avoid unnecessary run-ins with the clients. In their ideal world, the Agency would stuff her down the chimney like one of Santa's elves, and make her go about her work undetected. Corazon stood outside the bedroom door, debating whether to knock. "We lost it, Mark," she heard Mrs. Hartman say. Corazon couldn't be sure but she thought she heard Mrs. Hartman crying, so she stepped away and hurriedly finished cleaning the other rooms. Mrs. Hartman didn't re-emerge, and Corazon could only hope that she wouldn't be held accountable for the day's unfinished job.

Corazon stepped back and looked at the photos again. She was finally satisfied that they all lined up perfectly. She had spent far too much time on them today. Much like the photo she kept with her at all times, in her apron pocket. She had even started bringing it to work lately. It was of Amanda and Robbie, her babies. They were standing in front of Corazon's grandmother's house in Mindanao. Amanda was wearing a pair of knee-length blue shorts and a *Dora the Explorer* T-shirt that Corazon had sent by overseas mail in her first year as a Live-In. Robbie looked well, but he wasn't wearing any slippers. Corazon's brother Edgar had taken the picture at her request. Truth be told, it was a terrible picture. The sun was too bright, the children were squinting, and they weren't even smiling. To make matters worse, her grandmother was standing in the doorway smoking a cigarette while looking away, most likely at the flowering banana trees or the mountain range behind her. Corazon only wanted a picture of the children to see how much they had grown in the time she had been away; her grandmother was an intrusion. And the sight of Robbie without slippers bothered her to no end. Was it too much to ask to take one decent picture, she thought sourly, thinking of her children growing up under her brother's guardianship. She had told herself their separation would be temporary. Just a few years as a Live-In, she rationalized. Then I can apply for permanent residency and bring the children. The argument appeared sound at the time. Only when the work visa arrived did Edgar finally acquiesce. He already had three children of his own so she didn't blame him for resisting at first. I can't pass up this opportunity, Edgar, she pleaded again. They're recruiting now. The Live-in Caregiver program is different. The government regulates it. And I have the right to apply for permanent residency after two years. Just two years, Edgar.

That was four ... *more* than four years ago, Corazon corrected herself. Amanda was seven when she left and Robbie was only three, likely the same age as the little girl in Mrs. Hartman's photo. She was still haunted by the image of him fighting to untangle himself from Edgar's grip. She imagined him crying every night. She couldn't remember when her own tears had run dry. Was it after their first Christmas apart? Or was it after Amanda's ninth birthday, when it was clear she wouldn't be able to go home for a short visit? *Maganda* Amanda, she used to call her when she was a baby in her arms. She was growing up too fast. Soon enough they would have to start worrying about boys. She wondered if Edgar was strict with Amanda, or if he was oblivious to the comings and goings of his children—her children.

She paused to catch her breath, tracing the raw edges of the photo in her apron pocket. I'm doing this for them, she reminded herself for what seemed to be the hundredth time that day. Some day they will understand why the years have dragged on. But how can I ever tell them about Mr. Lawrence, she cringed. His poor children had no one else to take care of them since their mother had passed away.

She had hated leaving them. But she had not come all this way to be treated like some mail-order bride. And would they even believe what happened with the Changs? she wondered sadly, pushing back a stray clump of hair from her eyes. That they almost killed me, making me sleep in that basement with hardly anything to keep me warm? It was the Agency that had made Corazon leave when Mrs. Chang complained they hadn't paid good money for a sickly caregiver. And yet, as bad as it was, she would have stayed with the Changs had someone only told her that leaving them meant starting back at zero. No matter who was at fault. No matter who broke the terms of the contract. No matter how loyal she had been to the Agency. None of it mattered. What should have been a two-year contract to live with one family had become a four-year period of living in three different households.

But that was the past. She had finally worked for one family for an uninterrupted and uneventful two years. Corazon instinctively reached for the crucifix pendant her grandmother had given her on her last visit, which now felt like a lifetime before Edgar had taken that photo. She kissed it in gratitude. She was free to apply for her residency now. Amanda and Robbie would be here already, she sighed deeply, but seven thousand dollars! *At least* seven thousand to sponsor the children, the immigration lawyer had told her. She would have to start saving every last penny. What this would mean for the children while they were still in Edgar's care, she didn't know. All her earnings went back to Edgar. It was the only way he agreed to look after them. If she didn't send the money home, what would become of them? Then again, if she didn't start saving up, how was she to bring them here?

After paying her dues as a Live-In, she begged the Agency to find her different kind of work. Please let me clean, she said, trying to assert herself like her roommates Marisol and Florence had instructed her. No more Caregiver, they told her. No more, she echoed, heeding their counsel. They had been here long enough to know how things worked. And they were right. She was one of the lucky ones now. The Agency assigned her to the maid service sector and she could work more hours if needed. And the best part was that she no longer had to live like an outcast among strangers, learn to cook food she'd never eaten, raise children whose million and one needs made her feel so inadequate. It would take her a little longer to save what she needed. But at least she had the dignity of going home to her own bed every night. It wasn't much: a cot in a one-bedroom apartment shared by four other domestics. But they were like sisters now. Bonded.

How am I going to save seven thousand dollars? Corazon agonized. What if I never have enough to sponsor them? The thought terrified her. But Corazon reminded herself that she had made her choice. There was no going back. Only forward to the day she would have the money to sponsor her children.

Corazon went to the kitchen, the room saved for last in her cleaning routine. She perched herself on one of the bar stools tucked under the kitchen counter, stealing a moment to rest her legs. She took out the wrinkled photo wedged in her apron pocket and placed it on the counter, gently ironing out the creases with the back of her hand. How small Robbie looked. Would he even remember her if she went back home now? The last time she called home she couldn't hear him yelling in the background to his Uncle or big sister to let him speak to his Mommy, as he used to. In fact, Edgar had practically begged him to come to the phone. And Amanda was so distant. Worse: she was stiff and formal. Like she was talking to a school teacher with her mechanical responses of *hindi-po* this and *salamat-po* that. As though Corazon had become some estranged aunt the children were forced to speak to on their birthdays. She had talked to them every other Sunday for the past four years. In the first year, even if she was a minute late in calling they would get so upset. How much they cherished those few short minutes. *Mahal kita*, mama, Robbie would rush to say before the pre-paid phone card ran out, breaking Corazon's heart into a million little pieces. Maybe the next time we talk it will be like it was again, she muttered to herself.

Corazon took out the assortment of sponges and rags she cleaned the kitchen with and busied herself with her chores. Work was a relief at such times. She simply kept her mind focused on the mundane tasks at hand: wiping down a set of canisters with her microfiber cloth reserved only for delicate items. Scrubbing the grout in the glass tile backsplash with the S.O.S. pads she used in spite of instructions to the contrary. Straining to clean the hard-to-reach places, like the half-inch gap between the stove and the cabinets. Lifting the toaster to remove the crumbs lying under it, Corazon thought of Mrs. Hartman. How clean and uncluttered her life was. Everything had its place, everything had a purpose, like the various plaques in her home office arranged in chronological order along a floating shelf. Corazon liked to read them out loud to improve her accent: "Best Paper by a Psychiatry Resident, 1999." Or "Special Recognition. Canadian Psychiatric Association, 2009." Once Corazon even stopped dusting to read the first few pages of Mrs. Hartman's new book. She knew it was hers because on the top page of a large stack of papers she read "Dr. J. Murakami-Hartman," and the word "title" with a large question mark by it in red. Corazon realized the stack of papers was still there, in exactly the same spot on the desk where she had noticed it all those months ago. The question mark was still there too.

Corazon took stock of the kitchen and approved of her day's efforts. Everything sparkled, and she was always pleased when the pine-fresh scent of the floor-cleaning product permeated the condo, like incontrovertible proof of a job well done. Corazon liked that expression: a job well done. It reminded her of Mrs. Hartman. "Since I'm rarely here to thank you in person," she had explained, giving Corazon a box of pastries, "consider it my way of saying thanks for a job well done." Since that day, Mrs. Hartman had started leaving a box of pastries for Corazon in the fridge every Monday. It gave her something to look forward to at the end of a long day. And Mondays were always the hardest, when she felt her children's absence the most, as if speaking with them the night before only made things worse.

Corazon scanned the contents of the fridge. Some days Mrs. Hartman left chocolate éclairs. Some days a colourful mix of frosted cupcakes that looked too pretty too eat. If only the Agency had sent me to someone like Mrs. Hartman all those years ago. Things would be different now.

Corazon looked over the fridge again, hoping to spot a pastry box tucked somewhere in its recesses. Not once had Mrs. Hartman forgotten her little gift of something sweet.

Corazon moved a dish of leftovers to the side, thinking that Mr. Hartman might have pushed the package to the back of the fridge by mistake. Then she took out a few of the larger items, including a bottle of mineral water and a carton of organic eggs, to search the back of the fridge. She came across several slender boxes stacked on top of one another, and took one out to examine it. Mrs. Hartman's name was on it. Farther back she found a paper bag that contained several sealed syringes. Corazon recalled the day Mrs. Hartman locked herself away in her bedroom. She had been so focused on getting her job done that it never occurred to her that Mrs. Hartman might be sick, her mind now leaping to all kinds of morbid possibilities.

Distracted by her discovery, Corazon gave up on finding her Monday treat and hastened to put everything back in the fridge. Focused on the task of ensuring the medications were placed in the exact place in which she'd found them, Corazon forgot to pick up the wrinkled photo of her children from the gleaming kitchen counter.

\*\*\*

Janet Hartman dexterously rummaged through her purse for her house keys with one hand, the other holding a large white paper bag filled with medications. How had it come to this? she asked herself, fighting back a tear.

When she opened the door she was assaulted by the pine scent that usually lingered for hours after Corazon's Monday cleanings. She hated the artificial scent but didn't have the heart to tell Corazon. Today it was particularly overpowering. "I have to leave a note for Corazon to stop using that toxic product once and for all!" she mumbled crankily, dumping the bag of medicines on the console table in the foyer.

Janet massaged her right temple as she dragged her feet to the living room couch. She had a splitting migraine after having spent the morning rushing to the clinic for another round of blood tests and ultrasounds, the usual protocol of daily testing that came along with every new cycle. The late afternoon sun refracted through the floor-to-ceiling windows. She shaded her eyes with the back of her hand to block out the view. She and Mark had loved spending their evenings unwinding with a glass of wine as they watched the sky turn pink and purple against the blues and greys of the North Shore mountains. Now she couldn't look at the view head-on much less enjoy a glass of wine. It might interfere with the absorption of the medications, they said.

She had made so many changes already. Loading up on herbal supplements. Cutting back on meat and dairy. Giving up her daily runs around Stanley Park for a more low-key workout. Rearranging her life around the rigorous testing as well as the injections she had to self-administer with clockwork precision at certain times of the day. She hadn't even had the time to absorb the sobering diagnosis before she was thrown into an intensive treatment program, the likes of which even she, a medical professional, could not have anticipated. To make matters worse, the first cycle had ended in failure. Poor responder, they labeled her, because the dosage didn't have the desired effect. Someone needs to give those specialists a lesson in positive psychology, she thought irritably. Poor responder or not, she was convinced she wasn't that far gone.

How could she have been so wrong? she wondered, her gaze fixated on the black and white photo of her grandmother on the top shelf of the built-ins. "If you want to continue the treatments we can," the doctor had said with practiced indifference. They both nodded in the affirmative without so much as looking at each other. Did they *want* to continue? What choice was there but to continue? Janet felt a terrible pressure mounting behind her right eye. She had tried so hard not to indulge in worst-case scenarios. And yet here they were, facing the inconceivable.

She reminded herself of her training. Of what she'd counsel her patients to do when they showed signs of hopelessness or defeat. It was one of the first five steps in the ten-step program outlined in her new book. The peer reviewers had called it a ground-breaking contribution to the field. Surely that was worth something.

Close your eyes, she'd tell her patients. Turn away from the past. Then imagine a future uncluttered by present desires. Imagine something entirely new for yourself there. Janet closed her eyes, trying to move past the clutter. She remembered the day she won first place at the intramural Cross Country championship in her sophomore year. Running was the only competitive sport she enjoyed. She loved the singularity of the race. The sublime connection to one's own heart, the only thing one could hear during the intensity of the run. The power of the mind in plain sight. How even the most transient thought could make the difference between reaching the finish line or stopping dead in one's tracks. And the anatomy of potential. When every step expanded a muscle, contracted a tendon, re-defined the contours of mind, body, and soul. All those years of training, of discovering the pathology of her stops and starts, had brought her to this point: the 42K marathon she had signed up to run in the fall. She was in the best shape of her life. Yet here she was with a fridge full of medications. Advised to pull out of the race. Too much strain on the body, they cautioned. "You don't want to take any unnecessary risks, do you?" the Nurse had said, adding her two cents worth.

Janet closed her eyes again, disappointed that she was falling into the trap she coached her patients to avoid. Stumbling through the clutter of the past. She willed herself to take a deep breath and try again. She remembered the first time someone referred to her as "doctor." Doctor Murakami, as her patients and colleagues called her before Mark came into her life and she became Doctor Murakami-Hartman. How much she had wished her father were alive to see his daughter become everything he had wanted his son to be. If only he could have seen the name plate on her office door. If only he could have been there to celebrate the opening of her first private practice. Fully licensed and ready to *un*-do some damage, she had joked on the day she was to be handed the keys to her newly leased clinic. When she got there, Mark was waiting for her outside, grinning from ear to ear, an oversized red ribbon tacked onto either side of the locked door, and a bottle of champagne and two paper cups in hand. He understood what it meant: to be the first one in her family to have a bonafide profession—a *Canadian* professional with a *Canadian* degree.

Janet smiled, the tension in her head and neck easing ever so slightly. The champagne reminded her of the day Mark proposed. Not because he had made a show of it. In fact, by his own admission the question seemed to be pulled from the sky, impulsively, if not a bit clumsily. Signature Mark, she thought.

She closed her eyes again. They were driving home from her grandmother's house. Janet wanted Mark to meet her before it was too late. How much she missed Grandma Emi, Janet thought, suddenly overcome by the various absences that seemed to govern her life these days. At least Mark got to meet her, she consoled herself. How smitten with her he was! So much so that she teased him endlessly about whether he was sure he had proposed to the right Ms. Murakami. Janet learned more about her grandmother in those few short visits with Mark than in an entire lifetime of family exchanges. It wasn't as if she was in the dark about their history. Everyone in the family looked up to Grandma Emi. It's just that she had never opened herself up like that before, telling them stories that she had kept tucked away, so close to her heart, all these years. She had never talked much about what those early days in Canada must have been like, with a relative stranger for a husband and an equally daunting set of unknowns threatening to turn her into a stranger in her own eyes. Grandma Emi was never the type to kowtow to anyone, but to this day she wouldn't take any credit for having made a success of the family business, even though Janet knew she was the one who balanced the books, who had the confidence to speak to the suppliers in English, who made sure they weren't being cheated, who welcomed outsiders, and tripled their clientele.

Mark proposed on the day of their third visit to Grandma Emi's, a few months before she died. After they left Grandma Emi's, Mark insisted they go for a walk in the park. He wanted to see the Cenotaph memorial, he said, remarking on how many times he had walked by it without pause. Like the government apology for the internments, it held little meaning for him. He wanted to see it with new eyes, he said breathlessly. Grandma Emi's, he added.

As soon as they pulled into Stanley Park, the rain came down hard. People walking their dogs or taking leisurely strolls ran to take shelter under whatever tree or awning they could find. She and Mark decided to wait it out in the car. A full twenty minutes passed and Mark was still blathering on about Grandma Emi. Asking her to fill in the blanks about her family history, about her grandparents' return to Vancouver from Manitoba during the Repatriation period, a time about which even Janet knew so little because her mother had either repressed those memories or simply refused to grant her own children access to them. When Janet suggested they give up on the idea of a walk and go home, if only in the attempt to change the subject, Mark popped the question. Later that night when they were celebrating over a bottle of champagne, he said that the proposal just tumbled out of him, like the rain. Like the rain? Janet mocked affectionately. Could there be anything less *un*expected than the Vancouver rain?

Janet felt the pressure in her right eye resurfacing. How much had she done, how much would she be willing to do, to make this happen? No matter how hard she tried to visualize an alternate future, a space beyond the one outcome she longed for, she couldn't.

Janet closed her eyes again, sorting through the clutter, pushing it away. Her mind settled on the recurring fantasy of herself at a book signing, or the morning she would wake up to her name on the top of the *Globe and Mail*'s Non-Fiction Best Seller list. But the book was a done deal. She had written the last word, secured a contract, read and re-read the final proofs till three-hundred pages blurred into one. There was really nothing left to do but come up with a title. How had she let the manuscript sit on her desk, three weeks past the publisher's deadline, agonizing over one minor detail? Why was she so hesitant to commit to something as meaningless as a title? She promised herself to settle on something catchy but sufficiently academic by week's end.

It's time, she realized, looking at her watch and making her way to the kitchen. Taking out the syringe kit and medications from the back of the fridge, she placed everything she needed on the countertop, pleased that at least on Mondays she didn't have to go through the additional step of disinfecting the counter-top since Corazon had already scrubbed it clean, a time-saving gesture not lost on Janet. Corazon wasn't their first house cleaner but she had turned out to be their best, Janet thought, pleased she had listened to a friend's recommendation to use one of those domestic workers' placement agencies over the kind of exorbitantly priced maid services provided by the condominium board. Mark wasn't a fan of anything that smacked of migrant labour, but eventually Janet's "pros" had out-weighed his "cons." She had won the argument to use the placement agency just as she had won the argument to start these treatments.

Janet read the instructions again. "It's the maximum dosage," the pharmacist had said, far too ominously for her liking. Janet dismissed the remark. She needed to stay positive.

After self-administering the injection, Janet sat down at the kitchen counter, resting her head against her hands to stave off a dizzy spell. A wrinkled photo caught her attention. It didn't look familiar. It certainly wasn't one of theirs. She would never let her photographs look so beaten up and worn out. Taking another look past the wrinkles and the blemishes, she registered an image of two children. They were standing in front of what looked like a dilapidated one-room house on stilts. The little girl was wearing a pair of knee-length blue shorts with a rather worn-looking *Dora the Explorer* T-shirt, and the little boy was standing with bare feet. Janet studied the photo more closely. She could make out the edge of a flowering banana tree at the left hand corner. On the right hand side, she could see a bit of the landscape behind the shack. It was a mess of the deepest greens in a mountainous terrain. Moving past the dense foliage, her eyes landed on an old woman in the doorway. She was smoking a cigarette and looking away. Then Janet let her gaze rest on the children themselves. There was something vaguely familiar about them.

She turned the photo over to see if anything was written on the back, in search of some kind of verification in spite of the fact that the resemblance between mother and child was evidence enough.

Corazon's children. The words fell out of her like an indictment made for the benefit of the humming fridge and the elderly woman trapped in the image, her only discernible judge and jury. They seem so far away, she thought, following the line of one of the creases in the image with her finger.

Janet stood up and felt the room spin. She ignored the sensation this time, her energy consumed by the weathered photograph. She grabbed it off the kitchen counter and opened the one drawer in the house left disorganized by design. A packet of picture hanging nails spilled its contents into the drawer when she yanked the box of envelopes crammed under it. She made a mental note to tidy it up later, as she freed one of the envelopes from the box and scribbled Corazon's name on it. She did her best not to look at the photograph before placing it in the envelope—did her best not to let the sight of the children throw her off balance.

She walked over to the console table in the foyer, looking for a spot where Corazon would be sure to see the envelope on her next visit, relieved that it was the week of her additional Friday cleaning. She settled on the jade elephant a friend had given them as a ten-year wedding anniversary gift.

It would not do for Corazon to leave it behind again, she thought, feeling pushed to the limit. She propped the envelope against the elephant's raised trunk but it fell face down, refusing to stay in position.

Janet was about to prop it up again when she felt another dizzy spell. She reached for the wall, dislodging one of the black and white photos above the table. She didn't notice it had shifted off its right angle.

She took her hand off the wall in the effort to regain her equilibrium, at least just long enough to try to rest the envelope against the elephant again.

She was determined to make it work this time. She was determined to make it work.

# TORONTO'S DOMINIONS

LATA ARJUN MALHOTRA, née Lata Menon, cursed her Acura RDX for getting stuck in neutral when she pulled up to her Greater Toronto Area townhome. "Neutral? Seriously!" she whined, thinking of the argument she had with her husband that morning, one that she was determined to resume the moment she set foot in the door.

Accustomed to weighing success and failure in the language of finance—a trait compounded by her position as the Investment Relations Manager at a Mississauga branch of Toronto Dominion Bank—she lamented the bear market into which her life had plunged since the Menon-Malhotra merger. So much for sound record management, she thought bitterly. An otherwise prudent R.K. Menon had unwittingly plunged his daughter, hennaed hands and feet first, into a marriage that ruined her market value with every day that she bore the dubious title, *Mrs. Arjun Malhotra*. Somewhere between the crossing of the Indian Ocean and the Atlantic, R.K. Menon's investment into one hundred percent Brahmin stock, imported from the finest ports of his native Hind and selected among the old-moneyed echelon (a rare commodity amid Delhi's steadily growing bourgeoisie), had crashed to Titanic depths.

Sure, Arjun's parents had tried to sweeten the deal like condensed milk drizzled on a saltine cracker. They had generously offered to waive her dowry, a custom that her uptight cousin in Vancouver referred to as the reason why millions of female fetuses ended up in Indian landfills, but which Lata thought of as an unimpeachable tradition designed precisely to protect a woman's worth. Her father refused the offer, but begrudgingly made a show of accepting the Malhotras' contribution to other matrimonial expenses. Still, by Lata's calculations, a Toronto wedding paid for in dollars (while Canadian and American currency were on par, to boot!) versus a Delhi reception paid for in *rupees* hardly made for a fair rate of exchange. At least her gifts, which included a mini Fort Knox of gold coins (the new alternative to the conventional bangle set), was some compensation for the gross depreciation of what her father fondly referred to as his "best loved investment portfolio."

But then again, her father could not have foreseen, nor would he be able to compute, the extent of his recent miscalculations. Only Lata could project future contractual demise without the cushion of enough hurricane bonds to ride her through this emotional tempest. Only Lata could see bullion and bangles resold (though admittedly the gold market had never been hotter), and dreams of prime real estate holdings in Credit Mills forfeited, in the dissolution of a marriage that would bear little yield in terms of present family interests or future family gain.

For once she had seen the value in home-grown and homespun and *this* is what she had to show for it! He played a good game but *Made in India* he certainly was not! He had said the requisite amount of *pleases, thank yous,* and *namastes* to her parents. He had appeared adequately enthusiastic without being inappropriately desperate at the prospect of his Canadian bride-to-be. And his web-profile photos, which Lata had found particularly appealing, weren't airbrushed or doctored in any way (she knew this because she hired a fashion photographer to scrutinize them). And for all that, something had gone terribly wrong in the voyage across. Arjun was like one of those disappointing shipments of grown-for-export mangoes: touted as nothing less than the *Alfonso*, the king of the mango, when in reality he was as green and sour as the inferior kind used for pickles and chutneys.

Giving up on the unrelenting gear shift, Lata sat in her car and replayed their "talk" over and over in her throbbing but perfectly butterscotch-highlighted head of hair. And to think that all she'd said was that it was time to start a family.

"An heir! You want an heir! You can't have an heir without an inheritance!" he jeered, and stormed out of the house to catch the eight a.m. bus, which he insisted on taking because it allowed him to connect with the people. Lata may not have understood her husband's desire to connect with the people, or who exactly "these people" were, but it didn't take an expert to figure out that she had been struck out by a curve ball aimed and fired, with barbaric accuracy, at her total net worth.

Lata's first instinct was to scold her parents for not having done a thorough background check on the Malhotra family. Weren't they supposed to come from a long line of well-placed Delhi stock? Wasn't Arjun's great-grandfather supposed to be related to that Nehru guy? Or one of those people her *abbu-ji* droned on about, lapsing into languorous bouts of nostalgia for what he called the "days of york" or "yoda" ... or whatever the hell those days were. At any rate, those kinds of connections didn't interest her. In her fragmented and scant conception of Indian history, Mohandas K. Gandhi and Indira Gandhi were some famously unfashionable married couple, and "Partition" was a bad word whose mere mention launched her parents into frenzied exchanges of Hindi or a complicit silence that only a long distance call or news of relatives could break.

At any rate, the real injustice was not the suspect nature of Arjun's lineage. She had wanted to say as much when she called her parents earlier that day. Not in the mood to endure a lecture, Lata only managed to mumble something about their needing to be prepared to take some responsibility for this *hungama* before she, herself, hung up. Apparently her mother didn't dwell on the cryptic or frantic nature of the call, otherwise Lata would have been bombarded by ariatic voice messages all day long: "What is all this nonsense, *beti*?" or "How dare you hang up on your mother!" or the classic, "What will your father say?"

In retrospect, even her mother's tirades would be a welcome intrusion if it meant being able to confide in someone. She wasn't able to concentrate on much else anyway. She was desperate to confide in one of her co-workers but Lata had vowed, from what seemed to be her kindergarten days, to keep her Indianness, and everything that was remotely connected to it, where it belonged: in the *haldi*-infused walls of her mother's kitchen. In this she was sorely out of step with the times because, in fact, there was nothing hotter or cooler than being Indian, at least when it came to food and fashion. If she were a silk scarf, a beaded "tunic" or a foodies' secret ingredient in one of those *Top Chef* cook-offs, being Indian wouldn't feel so lame. But even in the category of consumable India, she felt like an outmoded spice-mix packet for some generic dish (*Vindaloo* or *Chana Masala*) upstaged by the fusion-inspired *Naan* pizzas or just-add-water exotic *Tamil* soups.

In spite of this, or maybe because of this, everything about Lata's life, except her arranged marriage, was a testament to her judicious adherence to North Ameri-*khana* (a bilingual pun that Arjun had invented in his mimicry of her decidedly *un*-ethnic eating habits, which generally consisted of boxed greens accompanied by broiled chicken breast or baked salmon). All her daily lifestyle choices were motivated by her desire to emulate the signs and symbols of a thoroughly Canadian existence that did not require the numerous accommodations of multiculturalism or political correctness. For this reason, the only person outside community circles who was privy to what Lata cryptically referred to as "the details" was her best friend Vanessa. And Vanessa had only found out because her mother once saw fit to entertain her with stories of the various "duds" they had rejected from the matrimonial websites. "I'm sorry?"

Vanessa had interjected, always a little discomfited by Lakshmi Menon's accent. "Duds, *beti*, duds!" her mother persisted.

"You mean *dudes*, Mrs. Menon?" Vanessa looked perplexed.

"No, duds, Vanessa dear! It's an Eng-u-lish word for ... *loos-ah*." her mother drawled, pleased with her efforts at crossing this idiomatic and generational hurdle.

Vanessa took a few minutes to decipher her mother's explanation: "Ooooh, you mean a *loserrr*?" Lata almost died having to sit through those excruciating eleven minutes till her mother shuffled off to tend to some household chore.

For everyone else, Lata had spun, with minimal gesticulatory verve (she was very conscious of the fact that *Desis* spoke with their hands), a mundanely credible fairy tale about meeting Arjun at a trendy nightclub in Delhi during a summer vacation. "First it was a summer fling. Nothing more," she'd breathlessly explained to Jennifer and Becky, the bank tellers she usually had lunch with. "But even with an ocean between us, we couldn't stop thinking about each other.... " Everything but the wedding details was sheer fabrication, of course, details which, in this case, Lata described with gusto, throwing in, for added visual effect, a few gratuitous comparisons to her ever-growing list of wedding-themed chick flicks: *My Best Friend's Wedding, Wedding Planner, 27 Dresses, Something Borrowed.* Not that Jennifer or Becky needed any cinematic assistance in imagining the scope, scale, and expenditure of a respectable wedding. Working at the bank was exposure enough. So many young couples were in debt because of their "big fat weddings" that one of the rotating managers had designated it a new type of "unsecured loan."

As for the divorce Lata was now bracing herself for: well, now there was a fine North American tradition she could participate in without any need for creative dishonesty. Maybe it would even help her bond with Jennifer, who was a twenty-something divorcée and single mother of two. Maybe divorce would give her the kind of edginess that twenty-somethings were supposed to emulate. She didn't know what classified as edgy, but she was convinced that making a mess of one's life was a sure step to gaining "street cred," a term she had picked up watching some reality cop show with her younger brother Sanjay.

Still hesitant to confide in Jennifer or Becky because of the million and one questions it might generate, Lata thought of Priya, the bank receptionist. In normal circumstances, Lata avoided Priya like the plague, but desperate times called for desperate measures. For one, Priya was the only one of her co-workers to have met Arjun. Lata recoiled from the memory. She had almost dropped the iPhone she was browsing with one hand, her custom-monogrammed water thermos in the other, when she saw Arjun and Priya chatting up a storm in the parking lot. To make matters worse, the two of them were speaking in Punjabi. Lata had no idea Arjun spoke Punjabi! She remembered being impressed by the fact that he had checked off the "fluent in multiple languages" category on his marital profile, which she assumed meant French and German, or French and Spanish, but as it turned out merely consisted of Hindi, Punjabi, and English. Another act of false advertising, Lata thought resentfully.

Lata seethed with jealousy at the sight of Arjun and Priya getting up close and personal. She was not only envious of Priya's universal claim to beauty, but also of the fact that the sum total of her parts magically transformed what was usually the vulgar language of race into the lyrical cadences of poetry: "Paki" metamorphosed into princess, "ethnic" into exotic, and so on. On most people that dreadful pierced nose would look so "yesterday," but on Priya it looked so "today" that Stella McCartney could have designed it! The colour-blinding effect of Priya's beauty on man, woman, and child—and even the occasional pooch—was nothing short of genetic larceny to Lata, who had never been the recipient of such flattering linguistic and cultural transmutations.

And to think that Arjun had made a point of saying that even though he liked all the pictures on her web profile, they didn't do her justice! That double-crossing, no good, *haramzada*! Lata fumed, as she feverishly scanned the bank's main floor for Priya while trying to erase the image of Arjun chatting her up in the parking lot like a love-sick puppy. Her only consolation was that Priya was newly affianced to that Dollar Store franchisee. Much to Lata's delight, Priya's engagement had set the rumour mill on overdrive because no one could believe someone as gorgeous as Priya would "choose" to sink so low. Even Lata did a double take: Dilip Singh? Of *Dilip's Buck or Two*? Dilip, the son of a Punjabi electrician and one of those weird Indian women from Trinidad? He was hardly a catch by anyone's standards! Lata clearly recalled the day she had become the unfortunate recipient of the wholly unspectacular account of the Dilip-Priya romance. "I was down to my last few pennies. And you know I have no experience outside retail. Then I applied for the position here and a cashier position at Dilip's store. Well, as it turned out I got this job too, but Dilip and I started seeing each other since my interview and the rest," Priya said with a twinkle in her eyes that made Lata want to stick her finger down her throat, "is history." *No doubt Dilip's a sleaze-bag and probably deserves to be slapped with a sexual harassment suit, but whatever,* Lata had thought at the time, bit her tongue, and smiled.

\*\*\*

"Poor Priya," Becky had muttered over her bagel and cream cheese during their lunch break earlier that afternoon. "I mean, having to spend the rest of your life with someone you, like, hardly know. That's too sad."

At that moment, Jeff, the office flirt who was, himself, usually two steps shy of a sexual harassment suit, sauntered into the lunch room. Giving the vending machine a gratuitous kick to release his preferred Mr. Big bar, he piped up, "Oh, yeah! What a waste. I give her two months before she needs a real man's touch, if ya' know what I mean."

"You pig!" Becky yelled after Jeff, though her smile betrayed her amusement.

"Grrrrr!" Jeff feigned a lion's roar coming in for the kill as he theatrically ripped open his Mr. Big.

"Cut it out, Jeff." Steve admonished Jeff mildly, as he waited for a frozen mac-and-cheese to heat up in the microwave. Lata sighed, transfixed by the bulging veins that contracted and pulsed in Steve's perfectly contoured forearms. It was no wonder she still found herself scheduling her lunch-break to coincide with Steve's, a habit she half-heartedly tried to break after marrying Arjun.

"Priya's only been here for a few years. She wasn't *born* here," Steve explained, bringing Lata back to the lunchroom chatter.

*Priya was ten when her family got here! She's as much a second-genner as I am*, Lata thought, piercing the slippery kidney beans in her salad bowl with added ferocity.

"You can't expect people to change overnight," Steve added. "We're talking about traditions that have been practiced for hundreds of years—for millennia, even."

Lata blushed upon hearing Steve defend her culture. Though she also smarted at his insinuation that arranged marriages were an antiquated tradition. Now she was more convinced than ever that she had made the right decision *not* to invite her co-workers to her wedding, even though she had desperately wanted them to see her all dolled up on the *mandap*.

"Speak for yourself, Steve!" Jennifer interjected while flipping over the glossy pages of an old copy of *Hello* magazine featuring the "Royals' Wedding of the Century."

"Or maybe Priya's the one who's got it right. I mean, the divorce rate is far lower in India than it is here. Being hopeless romantics isn't exactly a freedom we've put to any practical use, is it?" Steve persisted, directing his last comment to Jennifer, which Lata thought was a little below the belt.

"Hey, millions of people around the world celebrated the

royal wedding! And now they've got two royal babies!" Becky jumped in, though Lata wasn't sure if she was coming to Jennifer's or the royal family's defence. "Can you imagine, like, falling for some guy in your art history class and he turns out to be frickin' Prince William?"

"Don't be so naïve. It's not as if she didn't know who he was. Besides, people say her mother groomed her for the part for years," Jennifer retorted.

"Listen to you two," Steve interjected. "It's one thing for Brits to be sucked in by the monarchy, but what's our excuse? Did you know that the cost of that wedding cake you're looking at was thousands more than the combined pay increase of their entire cleaning staff at Buckingham Palace—a pay increase the staff never got. They're a tax burden, pure and simple."

"Blah, blah, blah," Jennifer mocked. "Don't be such a downer. So they had a big cake. What do you expect? A Sunday Special from DQ?"

"Didn't you guys learn anything from the Charles-Diana debacle?" Steve persisted. "And look how well that ended."

"Okay, man! We get the picture: you're hot for Kate!" Jeff cut him off this time.

"All this fairy tale crap has really got you people fooled. If Charles and Diana could have been an arranged marriage, then so could this. They've just got a better PR team this time round, so they don't look completely out of step with the times," Steve said, ignoring Jeff.

"Steve's right. It could have been an arranged marriage, like Charles and Di," Lata chimed in this time, thrilled that she was the one coming to Steve's defense.

"See, ladies? Kate and William; Priya and Dilip. Same difference."

Lata almost choked on her low fat pro-biotic blueberry yoghurt. Same difference? That wasn't her point at all. That was like comparing *The Bachelor*, the Rolls Royce of reality TV shows which she religiously PVR-ed because it fell on Spin

Class night, to *Bridezillas!*

When Steve and the others dispersed, Lata flipped through a more current version of *People* magazine featuring the "Royal Baby Diaries" devoted entirely to centerfold pages with Kate and William holding their first-born son. *That could be us,* Lata sighed enviously. She'd counted on becoming pregnant no later than their first anniversary, preferably around the holidays so she could make a spectacular announcement of their "Christmas miracle" over Turkey dinner.

\* \* \*

As soon as she unlocked the front door, she was assaulted by the unmistakable stench of hot dogs sizzling in a frying pan. She'd asked him time and time again to barbeque them outside, particularly because she was convinced he was eating the *all-beef* kind.

"For god's sake, Arjun!" she shouted from the foyer.

"And hello to you too!" Arjun shouted back.

When she entered the kitchen, he was fishing out the dogs with a set of tongs and setting them on a poppy-seeded bun. "Care for some dinner?"

"Gross!" Lata put her hand up as if to draw an invisible line between herself and the greasy object suspended in the tongs. Grabbing an anti-odour deodorizer, she proceeded to spray the room with vengeful zeal.

"Opening the window would be just as effective!" Arjun countered, while hunting for condiments in the fridge. He picked out a jar of Patak's Hot Mango Chutney, a bottle of Jamaican Scotch Bonnet hot sauce, a squeeze bottle of French mustard, and a Costco size tub of onion relish, all of which he placed together on the kitchen table.

"Well, that's how we do things in the *First World*," Lata retorted. "If you don't like it, why did you come here in the first place?"

"Why indeed? I should have stayed in India where there is

no shortage of jobs for someone with a Master's in Computer Science," Arjun said, spreading a heaping spoonful of the syrupy chutney on one side of the bun. "This is not exactly the IT mecca, is it? Why would I come to a place that outsources most of its jobs these days! The *First World* seems pretty close to bankruptcy, if you ask me."

Lata knew enough about market trends to admit that he wasn't entirely wrong. But she was more confused than ever about Arjun and his motives.

"So-why-then?" she repeated, slumping herself into one of the chrome and lucite dining chairs she had picked out in her mind well before she and her father had put a down payment on their townhome.

"For you, of course." He seemed serious enough but Lata wasn't about to fall for that again.

"You know what I'm asking. Why didn't you just marry an ... Indian?"

"I thought I did...?"

"I'm Can—" Lata cut herself off, seeing Arjun smile impetuously. "You know what I mean!"

Arjun seemed to be talking to himself as he contemplated whether to open the Jamaican Hot Sauce or the French Mustard first, settling on the former. "I just thought things would be different here."

"Different how?"

He took a substantial bite of his hotdog in a way that reminded her a little too much of Jeff. "Just different."

Lata groaned. She had looked for a husband on the other side of the world precisely because she didn't want "different."

"And what does that have to do with starting a family? All I said this morning was that it's time to have a baby!"

"Correction: you said it was time to have an 'heir'."

"You know I was kidding. It's just that the Royals are celebrating the birth of their second child and it's been on the news twenty-four-seven..." she said, hoping her added emphasis on "second" would have some effect.

"It is not just that, Lata. There are far bigger things we need to work out first. Tell me, how are we going to pay for this house? It is well beyond our means, do you not agree? And speaking of finances," he continued, licking a drizzle of the brownish sludge from the corner of his mouth, making Lata cringe in disgust. "Perhaps we need to talk about expectations in that regard also. I was under the impression that we would be discussing such matters openly."

Lata tried to wrap her head around how the "baby talk" had morphed into the "money talk." Anyway, what was there to talk about? She assumed he would just take over all the major expenses, especially when they had kids. It's not as if she was wedded to her career or the whole nine-to-five thing. And for now what the hell did he have to complain about? She earned way more than he did. He was hardly in a position to talk about finances. "So this is about money, then?"

"It is not about money. It is about being honest. About reality. Or how do you say it? *Keeping it real.*"

Lata was not so much listening to *what* Arjun was saying as she was listening to *how* Arjun was saying it, as if she were hearing him speak for the first time: the way he didn't use contractions, the formality of his speech, the extra emphasis he placed on 'a'—like re-aa-lity, as if every 'a' was an 'aha' moment. Who did he think he was, anyway? Oprah?

Lata shifted uneasily in her chair as she watched him take a last bite out of his hotdog, its medley of mismatched sauces oozing onto her designer kitchen table like it was an aluminum *thal* or cheap patio furniture. She knew he was waiting for her to say something before he got up and washed his plate and utensils by hand, which made Lata crazy because they had a state-of-the-art dishwasher.

Maybe she had got it wrong, she thought, softening to him again. Maybe he was just trying to tell her he didn't want to start a family before he was better off, financially speaking.

Maybe this was just the stubborn male pride her mother had advised her to be extra sensitive to. A little macho pride she could totally accept. "Did you want to get a real job before having a baby? Is that what this is about?"

"A real job? I thought I had a real job."

"Your Subway manager job? You're not serious…"

"I worked hard to get that job. You try getting employed with no Canadian experience. And what if I want to work at Subway for the rest of my life? They have great sandwiches and they help people lose weight." Lata suppressed a chuckle, fondly recalling how amused Arjun had been by Subway's ad campaign that eating more bread, of all things, would lead to weight loss.

"This is my point, Lata. These are the big things.… You can't even tell your parents what I do for a living but you want to have my children? It does not make sense."

"You don't make sense!" Lata threw up her hands instinctually and brought them down on the table with a thud. The Patak's jar fell on its side and rolled towards the table's edge.

Arjun grabbed it just in time it and placed it back with the other condiments. "What is it about me that does *not* make sense?"

Lata anxiously toyed with her iPhone, as was her nervous habit. "I don't know. Nothing. I mean, everything." She noticed three messages from her mother. How had she missed them?

"Just 'everything.' Like what?" Arjun needled her. He was far too calm for her liking. Shouldn't they be having a screaming match? Or calling each other names like those couples filmed on the nanny-cams on *Dr. Phil*?

"Well, like I said, I don't get it. Your family pursued this as much as mine. Why bother if *they* … I mean, if *you* didn't want this?"

"It is true: *they* really wanted this. But *they* did not marry you. I did. It was *my* choice. Did I come here kicking and screaming? And unlike you, I am not ashamed of the way we got married. I know you have not told your friends at the bank about me."

"What did Priya tell you? I knew she couldn't be trusted."

"Priya said nothing. In fact, all she did was sing your praises and talk about how much she admires the fact that you finished your MBA. She regrets not having had the chance to go to university." Lata didn't believe a word of it but before she had the opportunity to say as much, Arjun added: "Anyway, what is important is that I did not do this for anyone else's approval, so I certainly do not care about anyone's *dis*approval. I did it because I felt it could work out. I just thought things would be a little different here, that is all."

"I don't know what you mean by this 'different' business. You're the one who's turned out to be different."

"Perhaps we both had the wrong impression, then."

"Why are you making things so complicated, Arjun?"

"*I* am making things complicated? *I* am not the one living in a fantasy world."

A fantasy world? Lata wanted to scream. Didn't *Kate* have a fantasy? And now she's produced the future King of England!

Lata could not have seen this one coming: Arjun, her perfect Customs-approved match, was starting to sound a lot like Steve. It was one thing to drool over Steve, but to marry someone like him! That was a fantasy she had put out of her mind a long time ago.

"Please tell me what you are thinking, Lata," Arjun prodded.

*You want to know what I'm thinking? I'll tell you what I'm thinking*, Lata fumed. *I want a full refund with default interest for time and benefits lost, not to mention compensation for throwing me back into the marriage market at second-hand value! I want to sue for damages for what my father would call a shameful breach of contract! And while we're at it, I want my* abbu-ji's *money back!*

Lata dropped her iPhone into her purse and got up to go. She was already late for Spin Class and she still hadn't checked her PVR settings. Arjun had an infuriating habit of messing up the pre-set timers, and she was not about to miss the season finale of *The Bachelor*.

"Where are you going? Can I make you something else for dinner?" Arjun asked after her.

"I'm on a diet! And for God's sake, barbeque those grease-bombs outside next time. You're not supposed to eat beef, remember ... or was I wrong about that too?"

# SUNSHINE GUARANTEE

LUCITA WIPED THE residue of detergent from her hands on an all-purpose rag salvaged out of a spaghetti-stained napkin. She glanced at her chart, a list of check-outs she had to clean in preparation for incoming guests.

"*Dios mio*," Lucita sighed quietly, thinking of Señor Gonzalez' reprimand earlier that morning. *You've been late far too many times this month; another slip-up and I'll have to take action; if you think you're irreplaceable, I've got a filing cabinet filled with applications from younger workers to prove otherwise,* and on and on he had chided. He didn't seem to recall the eleven years of service she had already given the Siete Mares Resort and Spa, so named for the seven private ocean-front hotels dotting the Yucatán Peninsula. (Rumour had it Siete Mares was undergoing a numerical name change to reflect its recent expansion in Honduras and Nicaragua.) Some of her coworkers hoped this would mean promotion or relocation. Experience told Lucita that the only difference between these resorts and their working conditions would be the quality of air brought in by the Pacific or Caribbean seas.

"Excuse me!" a nasally voice called out. Lucita noticed a round, sun-burnt face emerge from the doorway of what she made out to be Room 23B. The girl waved a shampoo bottle in her left hand. Lucita understood the gesture and searched her cart for bathroom supplies. It was against hotel policy to provide more than one such complimentary item per day, a policy enforced by regular inventory checks at the end of the week. On the other hand, the staff were trained to always put the guests' needs first. Any complaints of poor service would reflect badly on everyone during upper management's annual review, which usually appeared in the month before high season. Were it not for the promise of increased tips they would all most likely have preferred a few extra hurricanes per year over the December-January high season and its *"no hay lluvia"* or "sunshine guarantee" policy.

Lucita first heard of this policy from one of the younger staff, a front desk clerk named Angélica who was working the graveyard shift while completing her last year of university. The phrase rained on Lucita's Catholic ears like an epidemic of locusts: *How can a hotel guarantee what even Jesus Cristo can't promise? Do they not realize that they are God's servants, not the other way around?*

Angélica chuckled at Lucita's naiveté, saying, "*Ay, no seas tonta*. Even one day of rain makes the *gringos* feel that they're not getting their money's worth."

"And what if it rains? What then?" Lucita pursued what seemed to her an absurd line of argument, but if anyone could help her make sense of it, it was Angélica.

"If it rains, they're just offered something free, like a day at the spa or a snorkeling lesson. You know how much the *gringos* love free stuff. *It is the religion of the consumer*, as Professor Hernández says. *Mira*: people like you think that nothing good comes for free, and working hard is the only way to heaven. But most people think that *because* nothing comes for free, heaven must be a place where you get *more for less*. And Mexico is where the *gringos* come to get more for less. I bet you didn't know you're already in heaven, Lucita. Now you can forfeit next Sunday's confession and live a little."

Angélica's cynicism notwithstanding, Lucita missed her conversations with her companion from Guadalajara. Angélica possessed the same spirit of contrariness as her own son

Miguel. *How perfect they would have been for each other*, she reflected wistfully.

"Why do we kill ourselves to earn a few measly dollars?" Lucita once overheard Angélica berate Carmen who had made the mistake of bragging about a ten-dollar tip she had received from an admiring guest. Carmen was hired to guard a small kiosk advertising local agencies and attractions, though she spent most of her day texting her boyfriend whom Angélica suspected was a small-time drug dealer who was dating Carmen for her hotel access pass.

"Why can't we value our labour in our own currency? Why can't our currency value our labour?" Angélica continued, unperturbed by Carmen's characteristic disinterest, as the latter pretended to busy herself with the re-organization of promotional brochures: boat rides through jungle mangroves; day-trips to the *pueblos*; submarine expeditions; "authentic" Mayan dance troupes; turtle farm excursions; water parks; nightclubs, casinos; something for everyone.

*Ay, Señor!* Lucita sighed again. *Mexico? Heaven on earth? If only! Is that why Miguel has left me? Is that why Ramón has left me?*

Her brother Ramón's migration "North" had cultivated in Lucita a particular fascination for Canadian guests who made up the bulk of their clientele. Sometimes she would steal a moment to feel a fur-lined winter boot or hat in one of their closets. These glimpses into another world reminded her of the early snapshots of her brother's family clad in oversized coats, misshapen woollen hats, and mismatched gloves, clothes that they had no doubt bought second-hand as ill-equipped newcomers. What struck her most about these scenes was not so much the snow that blanketed the city like a tired cliché, but the flushed faces peering out from long, hooded coats or so many layers of clothing that they reminded her of nuns in their habits.

"Shampoo, *por favor!*" the nasally voice called out again.

Lucita rummaged through her cart, relieved to find that she had not as yet utilized her week's quota. She prided herself on her ability to turn *less into more*. By God's grace, they had never done without, Lucita thought, stopping to kiss the pendant cross that was her only adornment. Even now, without her son's contribution, she stretched her meagre salary into something both she and her mother could survive on. She marvelled at her younger coworkers who didn't seem to care if they ran out of supplies, like they didn't seem to think twice about spending a day's wages on frivolities like nightclubs and an arsenal of electronic devices. Their defiance of management also unsettled Lucita. But she begrudgingly admired their unorthodox resourcefulness. When it came to hair products, they would save the empty shampoo bottles, and refill them with the cheapest local brand they could find. They did this with an almost scientific attention to the scent, colour, and texture of the hotel product, which simple deduction revealed to be a generic Mexican brand repackaged in Florida with the hotel's logo.

Even as far as a few doors down from 23B, Lucita could feel the crisp, cold air wafting out of the girl's air-conditioned room. She instinctively rubbed her warm palms against the gooseflesh sprouting on her upper arms. *If the canadienses expected a "sunshine guarantee," then why did they keep their rooms so cold*, she wondered. The rooms were so unbearably cold that she had taken to bringing a sweater to work.

"Champoo," Lucita smiled courteously. The girl snatched the bottle from Lucita, reciprocating with neither a smile nor a frown but some kind of facial twitch, which was promptly followed by a shut door.

Lucita returned to consult her chart. She had to make her way round to the rooms marked for an early group check-in from Québec. The group check-ins made everyone's day the hardest and longest. It was little wonder that Señor González was especially unforgiving on such days.

Again her mind strayed to the morning. Her tardy appearances to work were becoming more frequent. But what was she to do? She had no control over her mother's health and even less control over the increasingly capricious mood swings that overcome the elderly. There was no doubt that her mother's mind was taking a tumble down the muddy hill of life. She lost ten precious minutes every morning just trying to convince her that it was Thursday, not Sunday, and that Padre Lopez was not expecting them at *la iglesia*. And then on Sunday mornings she had to remind her that it was time to get dressed for *la misa*.

She had even taken to mistaking the neighbour's daughter Albertina—who delivered a weekly batch of homemade desserts—for the sister Lucita had lost during her infancy. Sometimes the memory lapses were so great that she would find her mother sending Albertina back home with *dulces de guayaba* and *plátanos fritos*, because they had been her deceased daughter's favourites. Lucita and Albertina went along with the charade to protect the old woman and themselves from further grief. And she was too proud to admit it, but Lucita longed for a sister, if only for the helping hand she'd imagine her to be. It was no doubt a selfish desire that sent her to many a confessional.

And the high season complicated an already difficult situation. Every night when Lucita returned from work, no matter how late it was, she prepared the next day's meals in the likely event that she was asked to stay on for a double shift. If this were not an exhausting way to end a long day's work, three mornings ago she missed her bus because she had to make a second batch of *tortillas*. Her mother refused to eat the ones made the night before, because *those tortillas* had been poisoned by the devil's hand, a punishment apparently meted out to mark the sin of "godless" grandchildren. Lucita retorted that for someone who seemed to be *enamorada con la muerte*, was not a poisoned *tortilla* besmirched by the devil's hand a welcome facilitator of what was, after all, her desired state? This of course had led to more outbursts, including her mother's favourite aphorism: *pórtate bien cuatito, si no te lleva el coloradito*. And any reference to devilish misbehaviour would predictably lead to her tiresome adulation for Ramón who, unlike *his ungrateful sister*, would have spoken to his mother *con respeto*.

Lucita wanted to point out the obvious: that Ramón lived at the other end of the continent; that in fifteen years he had come for a brief visit with children who only whined about the heat and the food and the accommodations; time he spent tracking down an old friend who owed him what Lucita could only surmise was some meagre amount of money; and his bravado about sponsoring his mother's immigration had never materialized. But Lucita dutifully prepared a fresh batch of *tortillas* with greater alacrity when she realized that her mother's remark about godless grandchildren was directed at Ramón's children, and not her own Miguelito.

*And today! Por Dios!* Today, her mother's appointment with her Maker seemed to have arrived without the devil's interference. She had fallen on her way to the kitchen and, for an excruciating moment, Lucita imagined a broken hip bone or a blow to some other irreparable part of her fragile body. Sometimes it was all too much to bear alone. *Things were so much simpler before*, Lucita thought. Now she even worried about the dreaded day she would have to arrange her mother's funeral alone, though her mother still held strong to the belief that a mother's burial was a son's honour, not a daughter's obligation.

At least at work she didn't have to concern herself with the morbid preoccupations of the elderly. All day she heard the delighted cries of children, giddy with the fun and games the pool-side animators designed for them. Or she was surrounded by her youthful coworkers. Girls with heads full of silly dreams, and young men free to turn their heads in admiration of abundant beauty. She loved to hear them talk in what they called their "twilight hours," those short periods of respite between shifts. At such times, their uniforms and unnatural smiles would be shed and they revealed themselves in partial slices of gossip and idle chit-chat.

There were the serious types like Angélica working to put themselves through university or to finance some entrepreneurial project: they begrudgingly suffered the humiliation of taking orders from children screaming for more ketchup for their *papas fritas*, or from their parents complaining that the rum-and-Coke had a suspicious abundance of Coke. Then there were the ambitious types who eagerly tolerated the abuse in the hope that they too might bark out the very same orders to a court of underlings someday. And then there were the types who endured, who quietly absorbed insult, rebuke, or even the monotony of the day simply because they had to.

She knew which type she was, but her only child Miguel was not so easily classified. Miguel worked as a driver for a tourist agency in Mérida. This he did for the same reasons as everyone else, yes, but also for his own reasons. In fact, everything he did bore an element of difference, a sign of independence that at times made Lucita nervous, at times proud, and at all times, uncertain.

"*Mi ángel.*" How she missed him.

He wanted to be an architect, of all things! She understood what it meant to be a doctor or a dentist, a teacher or a lawyer, even *el presidente*, but an architect? She didn't understand the appeal of such a profession nor what kind of life it would ensure for her son.

"Architects build, *Madrecita*, not destroy," he explained.

"Like the Empire State Building," she remarked, looking at a postcard that Ramón had sent them on a family holiday to New York. But Miguel had scoffed at the analogy. "Why do we always look outside ourselves for greatness?" And he showed her some colourful pictures that archaeologists had recreated of the ancient cities. "Before the *conquistadores* came," he said proudly, puffing out his chest like a *quetzal*;

as if he himself had been there to protect his city from what he referred to as "the worst tourists" they had ever had the misfortune of welcoming.

It was the same excessive pride that made Lucita wonder how long it would be before he'd quit his job at the agency. "Don't worry, *Madrecita*," Miguel would mollify her whenever she warned him to hold his tongue. "In what other job will I be able to visit Chichén-Itzá almost every day? If that means putting up with that *pendejo*, Jaime, then so be it!"

In her circle, nobody paid attention to a past that didn't involve complex family trees or even more convoluted feuds that spanned multiple generations. That was the kind of history she understood. But the ruined cities that Miguel adored and the tourists came in the droves to see—that was another kind of history she didn't feel any connection to. She could understand why they might be a curiosity, those funny looking pyramids that seemed to serve so little purpose. She could even understand why they might be admired for their unusual designs, but beyond this they had little meaning. To her, they were good for tourism, and what was good for tourism was good for Siete Mares, and what was good for Siete Mares was good for her.

But Miguel saw them through another set of eyes. Lucita once heard her son complain to his friend Salvador: "Jaimé would rather think of himself as a Cortéz than a Cuauhtémoc. That's Mexico for you. He doesn't even bring up the Toltecs when he's showing them Chacmool. Everything is just *Mayan this*, and *Mayan that*. Like it's all the same damn thing! Blood sacrifice and idol worship! *Que fufurufo es*! And he's the one with the archaeology degree. Five hundred years of imperialism and what do we have to show for it? Intellectuals like Jaimé!" Seeing his friend Salvador nod in earnest agreement, Miguel wiped the sweat off his beer bottle and continued: "Chichén-Itzá, Machú Pichú, Tikal ... these are the symbols of our future. Just look at Bolivia, Ecuador ... *Los pueblos originales* will decide what our future will be, not 'the Jaimés' of this world."

Lucita recalled the conversation with a certain degree of maternal awe, if not a little dread. It scared her when he spoke like this. She worried that he might have gotten involved with some fringe militia group. Her mother, on the other hand, had a different view of Miguel's fascination with the past. "*La brujería!*" she would holler at him. As far as she was concerned, the sites were laced with the hexes and curses of witches. If anything, she held Lucita accountable for what she called her grandson's obsession with "those pagans." Nothing good would come from it, she ranted. Though at some point in the tirade, the focus had shifted from Miguel's idolatry to Ramón's "godless" children. Still, Lucita had to give her mother credit for predicting Miguel's departure. Somehow she had presaged that her grandson's preoccupation with the past would steal him from their future.

Lucita's memories were interrupted by the sound of flip-flops hitting the concrete floor. As she looked up, a young couple rushed passed her. The young woman was in pursuit of the man. She held on to the unfastened ends of a lime green sarong, revealing a tall, slender physique and small, cupped breasts protruding through a skimpy bikini top. The young man's bare chest and legs revealed a golden matte of sun-bleached body hair.

With the English she had come to learn by osmosis, listening to staff interact with guests, Lucita made out the words, "Screw you!" As the young woman flew past her, a light spray of chlorinated water settled on Lucita's arms and face. She followed their trajectory to one of the rooms at the end of the open-air corridor. She had learned not to take playfulness for granted, as she had seen it turn ugly on many occasions, a tendency aided and abetted by what she considered to be the overly liberal all-you-can-drink policy included in the hotel's vacation package. How often had she had to liberate the rooms of plastic glasses reeking of tequila shots, margarita, and beer, remnants from the previous day's and night's revelries. The first thing Lucita did when cleaning rooms was open the windows to air out the combined staleness of alcohol and semen, mixed with the heady smells of deodorants, hair sprays, body washes, facial creams, and other lotions and potions for parts of the body she could not even identify. It was a wonder they used the complimentary hotel items at all, given the amount of products they brought with them.

Lucita stopped to see what the couple would do next, just in case security assistance might be required. Her concern dissipated when she saw the young man groping his shorts for his room key card while the woman, who had now caught up with him, slipped her hand into his bathing shorts and coiled her leg around his thigh. As they clumsily fell into the room, their lanky bodies wrapped around one another, Lucita remembered her early days at the hotel. She didn't think herself a prude, but no amount of *Salve María*'s could expunge the things she had witnessed here. These days, she did not even know which room belonged to which guest, because "partner switching" was, according to her co-workers, a new fad. And resorts across Cancún were promoting themselves as "adult only hotels," or "temptation hotels." Angélica once translated one of Carmen's brochures promoting a new Siete Mares affiliate where "sexual freedom was guaranteed under blue skies and a meridian sun."

Lucita couldn't help but wonder why the *gringos* came to Mexico for such freedom. Wasn't America the land of the free? But she knew it wasn't fair to judge only the *turistas*. How often had she found some of the married staff carelessly leave their name tags in rooms, which she would discreetly pick up and return to them. Sometimes she couldn't tell the difference between what she called "the visible staff"—the poolside animators, the fitness club trainers, the lifeguards, the bartenders—and the guests. They were usually lighter skinned, spoke English, and were generally perceived as untouchable, unlike the invisible army of chambermaids, security guards, busboys, gardeners, dishwashers, and sweepers, who were not meant to be seen. At least their youth and beauty brought them some benefit, Lucita would think to herself, neither in envy nor reproach.

Angélica carried those privileges as well, but she broke staff rank and fraternized with the invisible ones like Lucita. "See, Lucita," Angélica pointed out ironically, "we're lucky we work in a hotel that *only* guarantees sunshine." Indeed, it was a small mercy that Siete Mares still promoted itself with the slogan: "Sun, sport, and fun for the whole family." Not that such distinctions held any merit in reality. She had endured more than her fair share of inappropriate advances. If her husband Oscar were alive, he would certainly have disapproved of her job at the hotel.

*How much like his father Miguel is, and he doesn't even know it*, she thought regretfully. The conversation between herself and her son before his departure was as vivid to her as the last words she had shared with her husband before his death: "*Dime, hijo*! Is she from America? Are you going to join your *Tio* Ramón in Toronto?" To Lucita, Canada and the United States were interchangeable: both were "America" insofar as both were the land of the *gringos* in *el norte*.

But she had spoken in haste, forgetting Miguel's antipathy toward his uncle and his migration north. "*Madrecita*, Tio Ramón lives in the north but we all live on this continent, don't we?"

Lucita nodded in the affirmative, unsure how else to respond to Miguel's increasingly bewildering questions.

"*Bueno*! Then, we live in America too. This is *our* America."

He continued more soberly: "Besides, these are all just names. First Columbus and the 'Indies,' then Vespucci's '*nuevo mundo*' and then 'America.' All names. We live in the shadow of too many names. Names with power, but only so far as they trick us into seeing what isn't there—seeing borders and barriers where there should only be rivers and mountains. Like their new iron curtain, making a show of keeping us out when in reality they'd have no money to build those walls if we didn't work for nothing, picking their strawberries, cleaning their buildings, weeding their gardens, raising their children. Why do we continue to accept these illusions? Like that God you and *abuelita* pray to. All false! Designed to rob us of our ability to choose how we see ourselves. I'm tired of this place, *Madrecita*. I'm tired of believing in someone else's magic."

If she could have only made sense of all this; if she could have only found in these parting words an explanation for what she considered another abandonment, maybe then she would not resent this *gringa*. How many nights had she prayed, pleading with *La Virgen Morena*, mother to mother, to make her Miguelito change his mind and stay home ... to stay where he belonged.

Lucita wanted so much for him. *All that knowledge. Where had he got it? So much potential.* But for all of his god-given intelligence, he was not thinking straight. By his own logic, how could he explain leaving the land he defended with the conviction of *El Papa*? As much as she resented Ramón for leaving them, at least her brother's motivations were clear: he believed in the dream of *el norte*. But Miguel didn't want second-hand dreams passed down to him from the likes of his uncle. *At least one's own illusions are better than borrowed ones*, he'd say. Still, how was Miguel's dream any different from her brother's when it depended on another *gringa*'s charity?

Bereft of the insight she longed for, she could only surmise that Miguel had, in fact, fallen *in love*. There was no other explanation for such foolishness. Recalling the photograph of her son, his arm around a woman with pale green eyes and skin the colour of *tamarindo*, Lucita absent-mindedly dipped the spaghetti-stained napkin into a tub of polishing wax. "*Sopas!*" she muttered in irritation. Their smiles glared back at her in direct contrast to the sad-looking building they were standing in front of, long and rectangular, dilapidated and overrun by tropical vegetation. Miguel had scribbled on the back of the photo: "Sunita y Miguel en Berbice, Guyana. *Casados* en Georgetown, 5 *de Mayo*, 2010."

Looking at Miguel and then the woman standing beside him, alien but incontrovertibly beautiful, Lucita's skepticism re-emerged. For one, wasn't this Sunita "a cradle robber," a term she had once heard Angélica use to refer to an *árabe* from Brazil who regularly frequented the hotel with young *negritas* for companions. Older men with younger women; this was hardly a scandal, she had scoffed. The older Don and his doe-eyed virgin was the kernel at the heart of every *telenovela*—at least the types she and her mother watched, not the new ones about drug cartels in Colombia and Miami. And by now she was accustomed to seeing female guests in their fifties and sixties flirting shamelessly with the younger male staff. But Lucita couldn't imagine *her* son in such company, hungry for a *gringa*'s fickle attention.

When Miguel had said that Sunita was "a real Indian—like the ones that Columbus was looking for," Lucita was convinced that her fears about Miguel's embroilment in some Chiapas guerrilla force were warranted. Realizing he was talking about another country—other Indians—didn't come as much consolation either. "You're moving to India! It's too far, *hijo*. What do you know about this place? People are starving there; they don't have clean water to drink. You'll get killed or captured by the *terroristas*!"

"*Madrecita*: *de uno*, there's no war in India." He paused for a moment, as if caught out in a lie. He had, after all, just read a report about the Indian army fighting a war with a Communist group in southern India; it had caught his attention because they were referring to the fighters as *guerrilleros*. Deciding it best to keep such comparisons to himself, he continued emphatically. "And don't we have plenty of *terroristas* right here, like that

Mayor *abuelita* supports because he makes a show of giving money to the church during *Semana Santa*, the same money he gets from the drug cartel for his silence?"

Lucita chuckled. She too could not bear her mother's misplaced admiration for that upstart Mayor Velásquez. Everyone knew what a crook he was, wearing his notoriety like a badge of honour.

"Besides," Miguel added, "Sunita's never set foot in India. I told you she was born in *Inglaterra*."

"So then you're going to *Europa*?"

"Not exactly. I'm not sure."

Lucita's aggravation mounted. She was getting no closer to understanding what Miguel's long-term plans were. How could she reconcile herself to his new life if she didn't know where this life would be lived?

In an effort to reassure her, Miguel clarified: "For now, I am going no farther than *Sudamérica*. Sunita's great-grandparents were *emigrantes* who settled there. You could say that her family is as *Americano* as the *gringos* in *el norte*—as *Americano* as 'we' are! They've lived in the continent for generations."

"Then why doesn't she speak Spanish, *hijo*?" Lucita asked in earnest, trying to keep up with this convoluted family genealogy.

"That's a long history. But let's just say the Spanish got greedy and tried to grab too much of the continent for themselves. And eventually others grabbed what the Spanish couldn't hold onto. Why do you think they speak English in Belize and French in Haiti?"

"But what does that have to do with the *Hindus*? *Explicame, por favor*!" Lucita's head was spinning. She had never stopped to consider that Latin America could be anything other than Spanish.

Miguel scowled, recalling his embarrassment when Sunita expressed how peculiar it was for him to ask if she were a "Hindu" rather than Indian. He was not used to being corrected. Now he wanted to correct his mother, but decided not to complicate matters further. "*Madrecita*, aren't *Mexicanos* going to California and Canada to work in the *gringos*' farms? Well, long before the *Mexicanos* were doing this, people from India were coming here. People like Sunita's great-grandparents. They travelled thousands of miles to places like Suriname, Guyana, Trinidad. They came to work as *campesinos*. To carry the price of sugar on their backs, *Madrecita*, like the *esclavos* from Africa before them. But eventually, Sunita's mother and father left Guyana and moved to *Inglaterra*. That's where Sunita was born."

Hard work was something Lucita understood, so she momentarily dropped her guard. The *gringa* did look a little bit *mestizaje*, after all, which Miguel attributed to the fact that Sunita's maternal grandmother had a Portuguese mother and a Dutch father. This made Lucita consider the possibility that her grandchildren might have the benefit of being fair-skinned, after all—if, of course, this thing with Sunita lasted longer than the annual visit of *la mariposa monarca*. Upon further reflection, however, she concluded that any grandchildren her son might conceive with this woman would be as mixed up as their mother: her great-grandparents born in one end of the world, her grandparents born in the other, and she born in yet another. How could anything good come from all those separations? This gave her a newfound appreciation for Ramón's children: their insolence and entitlement might have been a source of aggravation, but at least they lived among their own, even in *America*.

Before she had the chance to point out her misgivings about future progeny, Miguel piped up: "Sunita has just come back to learn more about her great-grandparents' journey from India. She wants to write a book about them. She's a journalist. Not some *babosa* who wants to drink margaritas all day long and burn her face in the sun. I'm just lucky that she decided to visit Mexico for a few weeks. She didn't want to miss the opportunity to see Chichén-Itzá. Can you believe it? That's how we met: she and her friend asked me to take them back to Chichén-Itzá, because they didn't care for Jaimé's tour! *Créeme, mamá*: she's the right woman for me."

Lucita didn't know what to believe anymore. What did she understand about *Hindus* from Sudamérica much less *Hindus* from *Europa*? All she understood was that her son was more like his uncle than he wanted to admit. *If only Oscar were alive. Maybe things would be different.*

But it was too late. He had joined Sunita in this country she had never heard of. A tiny country in the South had entered her orbit, usurping the place that *el norte—America—*had dominated in her imagination for all these years.

She considered the photograph again. There was no accompanying letter. Still no indication of how long they would stay there. Or of where they planned to go when Sunita finished writing her book. And now they were married, but neither one had met the other's family. At least this kept open the possibility of a return.

A relentless Soca beat pounded across the resort. The music usually signalled the beginning of the day's activities: pool-side tanning; aerobics and salsa lessons; parasailing, deep sea diving and ski-dooing; facials and massages; and the ubiquitous drinking games, morning, noon, and night.

Lucita reached down for the detergents in the bottom tray of her cart. Straightening her bended knees, she walked slowly to the next room on her list, stationing her cart outside it. Here, she knocked twice, as protocol demanded, and then swiped her master key card through the electronic strip of Room 32A. The name on the chart read Célia and Pedro Ruiz-Caldéron, and Lucita was reminded of her brother's recently acquired "time shares" in one of the soon-to-be-built Honduras resorts, and his invitation for them to visit him there.

The only thing that seemed more absurd than the idea of her brother vacationing at such a resort, was the idea of herself as a guest at one of these hotels. What would *she* want in exchange for a rainy day? she wondered in amusement.

Remembering a childhood saying about the sun being the roof of the poor, she sang quietly: *Sol, solo te quedaste, de cobija de los pobres.*

As was her habit, the first thing she did upon entering Room 32A was open the windows, releasing the cold air trapped inside.

# BREAD AND ROTI

THE MECHANICAL RING of the toaster jolted Umara awake. She touched the side of her face, reminded of the pain. She turned her head and noticed a sparrow that beckoned from the balcony ledge of their ninth floor apartment.

Kashif, her son, came into the room carrying a plate with two slices of peanut-buttered toast. She couldn't understand how he ate that dreadful paste. It looked like mud and stuck to the roof of your mouth.

"*Ammi*, remember your doctor's appointment this afternoon," he said, sitting down on the recliner he had made a point of claiming in his father's absence.

She nodded slightly, the bare minimum of a gesture. It still hurt too much to talk, especially in the mornings before the day's round of medications kicked in.

"It's an important one," he added, just as his cell phone rang.

Umara didn't need reminding that today the doctor would tell them if she could finally be rid of the feeding tube inserted in her stomach. It made her feel like those factory machines.

"The news? No, I just woke up," Umara heard Kashif say to someone.

She turned to the television. A film had started playing on her favourite Hindi Classics movie channel. An impious looking man in a frumpy suit was heckling workers hunched over by the weight of large sacks of flour they were carrying up a winding hill.

"Again? I can't believe it!" Kashif's voice drifted over to her in heated tones. "Is anyone hurt? And the *maulana*? Was he there when it happened? *Khudah ke fazal*...."

Umara was taken aback by her son saying things like *khudah ke fazal*. He had never spoken that way. And why was he inquiring after a *maulana*? They hadn't been to *masjid* in years.

"Of course, I will," Kashif continued, somewhat flustered. "Please tell Ishaq-*bhai* I'll be there."

Ishaq-*bhai*? The name was vaguely familiar, but Umara wasn't sure if Kashif had mentioned it before or if she knew it from somewhere else. She was increasingly bothered by the fact that her son was spending less and less time at home, and more and more time going god knows where and doing god knows what. It was too much like the months before....

She felt the heat rise to her face. She was tired of the way the world kept sneaking up on her like a car's headlights in a dense fog. With every part of her anatomy hijacked by the cancer treatments, could anyone blame her for feeling this way? Didn't Kashif understand how little energy his mother had to be worrying about him too? She couldn't inquire about his every movement and action. Simply watching his comings and goings was enough to wear her out.

Umara sank back into the film. The South Asian channels helped her through days that unfolded with the certainty of sickness and inertia. Yet the monotony was enough to make her miss her job at the Ginetti Family Food Corporation. She even felt a brief twinge of nostalgia for Indira-*sahiba*, her disagreeable supervisor. At least Indira-*sahiba* and her coworkers at the bakery were part of something that was uniquely hers. After all, she had worked there for the last ... she struggled to do the math. Was it ten years? Twelve? Twenty?

"Too-too many years!" her Bangladeshi neighbour Nasreen-*bibi* used to say. "Umara, why don't you get a job closer to home. *Itni dur-dur hai*—so far on that bus!"

Easy for Nasreen-*bibi* to say, Umara thought irritably. Her uppity neighbour hadn't worked a day in her life. What did *she* know about what it took for someone like her to get a job? Umara would have been willing to accept anything—even working under the table, as Indira-*sahiba* had referred to it in her overly contrived Canadian accent. Had it not been for Nasreen-*bibi*'s husband, Zia-*bhai*, who liked to dole out unsolicited advice lest people forget he was a bigshot lawyer in Dakka, she would have blindly accepted such terms.

And what a thrill it was to receive her first paycheque, issued in the name of Umara Haroon Siddiqui. It was so official ... so Canadian, she had thought at the time. Even though she felt cheated by all those deductions, thinking that maybe Zia-*bhai* had misled her, the bi-weekly cheques made her feel like her own person. That's why the first thing that upset her about the cancer diagnosis was the prospect of losing her job, and becoming the government's charity case.

"It isn't charity, Umara-*bhain*," Zia-*bhai* corrected her. "It's *your* money. The hospital bills, the time off work ... you've been paying into those benefits all these years. Why do you think I told you to insist on doing things the right way?"

She couldn't get over how much she was itching to get back to work. But when? The doctor had said it would be quite a while before she was "out of the woods." The expression had stuck: when she looked at her reflection in the mirror she thought of a mountain after monsoon season: treeless, muddy, and beaten down by a landslide. At least that's what she saw now that a section of her tongue and cheek—or oral cavity, as they called it—was cut out to prevent the cancer from spreading.

"Can't let ... injustice ... something ... about it," Kashif's voice weaved in and out of the voices in the film: "*Bhookh laghe hai*! *Bhookh laghe hai*!" the frumpy man taunted the workers struggling not to buckle under the weight of those bags, their only path to a meal at the day's end.

"*Mein bookha hun*," Umara parroted the man in the film,

thinking of the few words Kashif's father would say in the months before he left.

\*\*\*

She stood in their small galley kitchen, kneading a fresh mound of dough. Once it had formed to the desired elasticity, she tore off a piece and rolled it into a ball on the lightly-floured portion of the kitchen counter. Then slap, slap, slap, she started to flatten it down with her hands, making it thinner and thinner as it hit each palm, back and forth, back and forth. She knew better than to make the chapatis too early. He couldn't stand it when she heated them up in the microwave. And he was right. The microwave made them stiff as a board, like those Ginetti biscuits. As soon as she got home from work, she would prepare the dough and leave it to sit in a bowl under a dishcloth, while one vegetable and one meat dish simmered to perfection on the stove. The last step of placing the flattened circles of dough on the tawa was reserved for the moment she heard him come in. She watched the chapatis bubble up on the iron pan. Then she picked them up, one by one, scorching the tips of her fingers. Each one placed lovingly in her favourite bread basket with the colourful tassels, one of the few things she had brought with her from Lahore. To think that the basket was now as old as their marriage, as old as their only child, already a teenager finishing his last year of school, and as old as the life they had built, more apart than together it seemed, in this new land.

By the time he had washed his hands of a day spent chauffeuring people around the city in his taxi, and seated himself at the table, a batch of steaming hot chapatis filled the apartment with the nourishing aroma of home.

\*\*\*

Umara longed for her customary breakfast of *roti-makhan-chini*, a warm piece of roti fresh off the *tawa*, with a dollop of *ghee* and a light sprinkling of sugar melting over it, but she hadn't made or eaten any kind of roti in months.

A weight pressed down on the sofa cushion beside her. It was Kashif rummaging around for something. She shifted her right hip, the slightest movement igniting little stabbing sensations on the right side of her face. The remote poked through a cushion, so she fished it out and handed it to her son.

He resumed his position on the armchair. "I have to change the channel, *ammi*. I can record your movie."

"Channel change *karó*," she managed to say.

Kashif was addicted to the news, Umara reflected, as the familiar chatter of the morning shows came on. She didn't mind watching the Canadian news now that so many broadcasters were South Asians. If she plugged her ears and only watched, she could almost be back home. If she closed her eyes and only listened, there would be no telling the difference between them and the *goras*.

*This is the second act of vandalism against the mosque. This time a burned Quran was thrown inside along with a letter, the contents of which have as yet to be released.... The police have only confirmed that the incident is being investigated.... In other news, stores are running out of Hunger Games costumes for Halloween faster than they can stock the shelves....*

A shaft of morning light illuminated Kashif's jawline as he leaned in to watch the news. If it weren't for the stubble on his unshaven face, he was a spitting image of his father. Haroon Siddiqui was a good-looking man. Everyone had said so at their wedding. The uncanny resemblance between father and son reignited the kind of silent glares and conspiratorial whispers from family and friends that had made her acutely aware of the obvious mismatch between husband and wife.

Kashif put his plate on the coffee table with a heavy hand and changed the channel back to the Hindi movie. Mehboob Khan, the name of the director, appeared on the bottom of the screen, as the scene shifted over to a palatial, marble-floored room where a stern-looking woman in a finely embroidered sari was scolding a household of domestic servants.

Umara didn't really like such old movies, but this one reminded her of the Pakistani films that were much harder to come by, maybe because they had more drama and dialogue than the flashy song-and-dance of Bollywood. The audio was a little shaky and the film was grainy in parts, showing its wear-and-tear in ways she could relate to. As if someone had pressed a fast-forward button the moment they stepped onto that plane, twenty-two years ago. As if their whole lives had just unfolded at some accelerated rate, with only the news of an uncle's death or a cousin's wedding giving her pause, giving her any sense of what made one year any different from another. The cancer was just another kind of accelerant. She wasn't afraid of it like some of the other patients seemed to be. If anything, the doctors were surprised by how stoically she was handling it all.

*\*\**

"*Are you a smoker, Mrs. Siddiqui?*" *Doctor Eleniak asked. It felt like an inquisition. She had never smoked a day in her life. She always rushed past the women smoking outside the bakery during breaks. She hated the way the odour clung to her clothes for the rest of the day, implicating her in their vice.*

"*Alcohol?*"

*Kashif, who not only brought her to the hospital but also agreed to accompany her to these appointments, answered for her:* "*We're Muslim. It's* haram.*"*

*Umara was proud to hear him say* "*we.*" *She didn't think he was a believer, tacitly having accepted Nasreen-*bibi's *reproach that the younger generation were losing their faith.*

"*Second-hand smoke?*" *the doctor persisted, looking at his notes.* "*Do other members of your household smoke?*"

*Umara pushed a stray hair behind her ear self-consciously, realizing whom the doctor was referring to. What was she supposed to say? That Haroon had neither smoked nor drank a day in his life, but had brought* gunha *to their lives all the same?* She exhaled with relief when Kashif took the initiative: "It's just the two of us."

"I see," Doctor Eleniak replied nonchalantly.

A litany of questions followed about her diet, all of which the doctor directed to Kashif. "Does she eat very salty foods? Preserved foods?"

"She makes all of our meals from scratch."

"I see.... And it says here that your mother works."

This time Umara answered promptly. Her English was broken, that much was true. She had never had the time to take those ESL classes way back when. How could she? She was pregnant with Kashif almost as soon as they arrived and then thrown into that job as soon as Kashif was old enough to start school. Besides, there was hardly any need to speak English at the bakery. Everyone spoke some level of Urdu or Hindi, even the Punjabi women who dominated the assembly lines. And although her husband used to take care of what she called the outside business, like paying bills or dealing with the landlord, she had picked up enough English by osmosis, through her son or television or those flyers that poured into the building once a week.

"I work at bakery. Since Kashif is five."

"It's not exactly a bakery," Kashif qualified. "She calls it that. It's a factory that manufactures Italian cookies … the ones that break your teeth."

"Biscotti?" Doctor Eleniak strained to crack a smile.

"Right. And other baked products like those funny S-shaped biscuits. It's Mom's job to do the sorting before things are packaged. Why do you ask about her job?"

The doctor mumbled something about the possible link between cancer and environmental hazards at the workplace, before turning back to Umara: "Mrs. Siddiqui, mouth cancer, in and of itself, is not that unusual. What is unusual is the rapidity with which it has spread through the right side of your mouth. There is a possibility that it may also have spread into your lymph nodes. The only treatment at this stage is to remove a section of your tongue and those affected nodes, as the case may be, after which we will have to give you an aggressive post-surgery treatment. Is this clear?"

Both mother and son nodded, stunned into silence by the prospect of such a surgery, the medieval image so out of sync with the polished surfaces, smiling support staff, and state-of-the-art equipment at the Princess Margaret hospital.

Doctor Eleniak glossed over their startled expressions: "Do you have any questions?"

Kashif was about to say something when they were interrupted by a hard tap at the window behind the doctor's desk.

"Bichari," Umara exclaimed.

"Excuse me?" Doctor Eleniak turned to Kashif again.

Kashif had also noticed the little bird fly straight into the window, but ignored it. "What about food?" he asked. "Eating?"

Doctor Eleniak cleared his throat and closed his file. "Unfortunately, it is likely that your mother will not be able to chew or swallow for a good long time after treatment. We will have to insert a feeding tube into her stomach to ensure she receives adequate nutrition. And I must caution that in some cases patients do not recover their ability to eat whole foods, and their taste buds are almost certainly compromised."

Kashif winced and looked at his mother: "Ammi, sab kuch samji?"

Umara was still focused on the window, only vaguely aware of the doctor's ensuing description of the months of treatment ahead. "Wo parinda kahan gaya hai?" she said to no one in particular, wondering where the bird had gone.

\* \* \*

Umara touched the side of her face, still unaccustomed to the sensation of flaccid skin. The medical team at the Princess Margaret were always so concerned about these physical changes, constantly reminding her of the counselling and rehabilitation available for patients undergoing invasive surgeries. But the truth of it was that she would not know what to do or say at such sessions. For one, all that talk about body and image made her uncomfortable. They would never understand that she didn't think much about such things. Why would she, when she had spent her best years covered up in a long factory coat, rubber gloves, and hair netting? When Kashif was younger, they had made a point of attending Eid festivities, which were always fun to dress up for, but Kashif's father's erratic shifts soon made attendance at the *masjid* or social functions increasingly difficult.

It was just as well, she rationalized, because she could not imagine having to face the community now. It would be like the wedding all over again. Only this time the judgment behind those silent glares would be that much greater. Still, she would be lying if she said she didn't miss the festivities, the sound of children shrieking with delight at the sight of balloons and colourful stacks of *mithai,* and the adults hovering equally excitedly over generous dishes of mutton *biryani, haleem,* and at least three types of roti.

Umara heard her son turn on the shower, and wondered where he could be going so early on his day off. It obviously had something to do with this Ishaq-*bhai,* another unknown that gave her pause. She wasn't about to lose husband and son to some other life. As much as she hated the idea, she considered asking Nasreen-*bibi* or Zia-*bhai* to help keep an eye on him, at least till she was back on her feet.

But any contact with Nasreen-*bibi* came at a price. First, it meant having to hear her neighbour's ministrations about this-that-or-the other. And second, it meant overlooking the fact that Nasreen-*bibi* had turned frosty since the truth about Kashif's father could no longer be contained. While this had not stopped Nasreen-*bibi* from offering assistance during the worst of the chemo and radiation treatments, her neighbour had made a point of sending one of her daughters to drop off food or groceries rather than make an appearance herself. Umara understood that Nasreen-*bibi* had her standing in the community to uphold, having always flaunted the fact that her brother was a *haji*, and some cousin-third-removed in England a celebrated *Imam*. Umara envied Nasreen-*bibi*'s piety, attributing it as the source of her many blessings, including three beautiful children: a son and two daughters.

Umara had always longed for a second child—a little sister for Kashif. She wondered what it would be like to raise a girl here. Would she turn out like Nasreen-*bibi's bachiyan*, their mother's little clones? Would she turn out like Abena, the daughter of her Sudanese neighbour Mrs. Osman, who had dyed her hair blonde and wore clothes so tight it was a wonder she could breathe? Or would she turn out like her younger co-worker Lailah in jeans and *hijab*, whom Umara likened to apple chutney, a strange adaptation of a familiar staple. After all, it was Lailah who raised the subject of Kashif's father as casually as a weather update, when Umara had done everything in her power to avoid the subject—to protect her family's *izzat*.

\* \* \*

*Lailah was running a little late. Umara didn't think too much of it till she heard her younger co-worker's voice soaring above the clank and drone of the machinery:* "Robbing us of a few minutes pay—that you have no trouble doing! But overtime for extra long shifts—that's too much to ask for," *she spewed.* "Don't think for a second that you're so untouchable! We all know that there are at least a dozen health violations you don't report, and we know that you convince newcomers to work under the table for whatever kickbacks you get in return. Do you think if the media got wind of a factory filled with minority women being exploited by one of their own, the great Ginetti family wouldn't hesitate to throw you under the bus? So go *ahead and dock my pay, Indira, or better yet, go ahead and fire me! It will be a pleasure to tell the Ministry of Labour all about your little operation here."*

The conveyor belts, oven fans, buzzers, and clanking robotic arms continued to fill the room with their mechanical noises, even though everyone had stopped what they were doing and looked on with bated breath. Much to everyone's surprise, Indira-sahiba *didn't lash back but merely fixed a steely gaze on Lailah as she walked toward her station next to Umara.*

"Arré! Who gave you all permission to stop working?" Indira-sahiba *eventually barked before skulking away into a stuffy storeroom she had turned into a makeshift office.*

*Everyone busied themselves again, making a show of being engrossed in the mundanity of their tasks. Umara was no exception, her hands at the ready to pick up anything that looked burned or misshapen. If the biscuit didn't have a perfect "S" shape or looked more brown than golden, it had to be discarded.*

*Lailah took her place by Umara's side, pausing to adjust the pins at the back of her hijab, and then threw herself into the same task. She didn't say anything until after the lunch break, resuming her characteristic chatter about the big university where she was studying subjects that made little sense to Umara.*

"To tell you the truth, Aunty-ji, I don't feel safe waiting for the bus after my evening classes anymore," *she said, referring to the escalation of sexual assaults against female students.*

*Umara nodded, relieved that the tension of the morning had abated. She was about to pick up the bin of rejected biscuits, now full to the brim, when Lailah poked her gently in the arm and, with lowered voice, said:* "Umara Aunty, can you stay behind a little before catching your bus? There is something important I have to tell you."

*Umara assumed this had to do with the big blowout with* Indira-sahiba, *and she didn't want to get in the middle of it. She had her job to protect. Especially now, when every penny counted.*

"*Aunty-ji,*" *Lailah prodded again.*

*Umara softened at the way Lailah called her Aunty-ji. It had a ring of warmth that was so unlike the way Indira-sahiba, who was no more than a year or two younger than Umara, derisively called her "Aunty" to emphasize the increasing slowness with which she went about her tasks.*

"Acha—jaldi batao," *she replied anxiously, looking around to make sure Indira-sahiba or her lackeys were not in earshot.*

"*Aunty-ji, you know how Indira was mad because I was late this morning.*"

*Umara shook her head from side to side in the kind of mild disapproval she felt it was incumbent on her to express, as Lailah's elder.*

"*Well, I lost it because she said I should stop waking up in strangers' beds. Can you believe it? That woman has no shame! I tried to tell her it was because I had to drop off a paper to a professor all the way downtown before coming to work, and she had the nerve to tell me that my ambitions are not her concern. ... Anyway that's not the point. The point is while I was there ... at the downtown campus, I mean ... I saw something. Or, rather, someone...*"

*Umara turned back to her task in annoyance. What had all this to do with her?*

"*It was him, Aunty-ji. Apka mian...*"

*Umara stiffened. How did Lailah know what her husband looked like? Then she recalled the time Haroon had to pick her up because the buses weren't operational during one of those terrible snowstorms, and she had insisted that he give Lailah a ride also.*

"*Aunty,*" *Lailah gently touched Umara's arm with her rubber-gloved hand.* "*I also saw him with someone. Gori ke sath...*" *Lailah leaned in and whispered as softly as she could,* "*Baby ke sath.*"

*Umara turned back to the assembly line and grabbed a handful of biscuits, including some perfectly good ones.*

"I'm so sorry, Aunty-ji." Lailah touched the top of Umara's clenched fist. "I didn't know he had left you."

Left you ... Lailah uttered the words so effortlessly—words she, herself, had been unwilling or unable to say out loud for the last six months. She couldn't even permit herself to say that Haroon had stopped coming home, telling herself that he had simply stopped coming home for dinner.

Umara pictured the scene Lailah conjured up on the bus ride home. Strangely, neither "the gori" nor "the baby" shocked her as much as the image of him spending time with this new family. What gave him the liberty to discover this country without her? Grey highways and strip malls bearing Indian grocers and Western Unions, or nondescript apartment towers, like the ones they were passing now—that was the Canada she knew. The factories viewed on her daily route, from Finch West to Woodbine—this was her orbit. And what gave this other woman the right to parade around with some alien version of her own husband? Apart from that one special trip to the CN Tower, a dinner in Chinatown for a few of their birthdays, and now her visits to the Princess Margaret Hospital, Toronto was as alien as "those woods" Doctor Eleniak referred to.

The opprobrious glares at her wedding came back to her like an eerie prophecy. There was so much temptation here. All these girls wearing so little—in sun or snow—with their spiky heels, and their figures bursting through the kind of outfits Mrs. Osman's daughter had started wearing. She imagined him talking to them in his taxi, especially late at night when they were drunk and felt less threatened by a brown man holding their life in his hands.

Umara didn't know what else to do but go on, as Indira-sahiba had done earlier that morning. How else was she to save face?

Months had passed since Lailah's revelation, but she held on to the information like a state secret, convinced that what she didn't reveal, no one could ever know. Convinced that the baby wasn't his and he'd eventually come home. Then Nasreen-bibi and Zia-bhai *started to keep their distance. By the time she was diagnosed with mouth cancer, she had not received so much as a phone call, and she was finally forced to face the facts. It was just the two of them now: mother and son. She consoled herself by arguing it had always been that way. Nothing she or Kashif did had brought him much joy. Even Kashif's birth had been a non-event, of sorts. He had simply looked at his son, mumbled something about carrying out the* manat *he had made at the mosque for a healthy child, and that was that. As soon as they got home, life returned to the routine of his extended absences. And her attention, at least, was consumed almost entirely by the child.*

\* \* \*

Umara vaguely registered a black-and-white image of villagers gathered around large mounds of freshly harvested wheat. One of the villagers, a tall man in a *lunghi*, looked down at the scene as he talked to the woman from the grand marble-floored house. The villager had just saved the woman and her husband, the owners of the city factory mill, from a near-fatal car crash. The man in the *lunghi* explained it was harvest time and everyone in the village would be given an equal share of the annual yield.

"Even the ones who don't work as much?" the factory owner asked cynically.

"Even them. No one goes hungry," he replied.

"Then no one is poor here?" his wife asked incredulously.

"Poor? I don't understand," he replied. Umara dozed off again, with the woman's derisive laughter ringing in her ears.

"*Ammi, mein bahar ja raha hun,*" Kashif said, gently tapping his mother's shoulder and pointing to the door to indicate he was on his way out.

Umara awoke with another start. She wondered why her husband was wearing that navy blue sweater—the one she had bought for Kashif last Christmas—when he had never approved of the gesture, saying it would confuse the child.

"*Ammi*, I'm going out!" Kashif repeated, picking up his cell phone from the coffee table.

"*Nahin jao!*" Umara shrieked, touching the side of her face to stave off the pain.

"*Fikur nahin, ammi*," Kashif consoled patiently. "I'll be back in time to take you to your appointment. Why don't you try and get dressed? It will make you feel better."

Dressed, Umara repeated to herself, realizing it was her son, not his father, standing over her and blocking the morning light. Why was Kashif always so insistent she get dressed? In fact, he seemed to be taking far too much interest in her appearance lately, asking why she didn't wear *shalwar kameez* anymore and commenting on the other women in the building who looked so smart in their traditional clothes.

Umara couldn't disagree. She loved the colourful head coverings and long embroidered gowns worn by Mrs. Osman and her Eritrean friend Mrs. Yusuf. They were so different from anything she had seen back home. Though, truth be told, she felt that Kashif was thinking more about Nasreen-*bibi*'s daughters who seemed unrecognizable these days, having forsaken baseball hats and hoodies for long-sleeved dresses and *hijabs*.

Umara heard the door close behind her son. The sudden emptiness of the apartment drew her attention to the bird's chatter, and the bread crumbs on Kashif's plate motivated her to heed the bird's call. A loose stack of colourful brochures fell to the floor when she picked up the plate. A few of them were from the Cancer Society of Ontario, which the doctor's receptionist had plied her with on their last visit. She had said something about newly implemented on-line chat groups, but Umara didn't know the first thing about computers much less what to say to perfect strangers.

Umara was about to throw the papers away when she noticed another set of glossy pamphlets from the Islamic Cultural Centre of Ontario. Immediately suspecting Nasreen-*bibi* as the likely source of such literature she was about to toss them aside, but the image of an impressive, modern building with mirrored glass caught her attention. The "new Islamic community centre" boasted the usual kinds of things, including schedules for Quranic classes, community events, and volunteer activities, but also unexpected things such as sports facilities and fitness studios for women, and even family counselling services.

She set the pamphlets down, a bit unnerved by the striking contrast between this elaborate complex and the dingy office building, with its musty carpets and cramped quarters, that had served as their *masjid* and community centre when they were new arrivals.

"*Bhookh laga hai, chota parinda? Bhookh laga hai*!" Umara called out to the lonely sparrow hopping from ledge to floor, and floor to ledge. She used the better part of her strength to slide open the patio door, just enough to extend her arm outside and unclench her fist, releasing the broken crusts.

\* \* \*

Umara stared idly at the Canadian Cancer Society poster mounted on the waiting room wall, hoping the distraction would drown out the television buzzing overhead. She liked the soft colours, and the yellow daffodils with the white centres reminded her of the pretty gardens they passed on their bus ride through some of Toronto's residential streets. Below the picture of flowers was a photograph of smiling people wearing matching T-shirts and holding up banners with the slogans, "proud supporter" and "celebrating survivors." The faces held little appeal so she turned her attention back to Kashif, who was on the phone with someone again.

"Have the police made any arrests yet?" His voice travelled through the sparsely decorated waiting room.

Umara noticed one of the patients, an elderly man reading a novel, shift uncomfortably in his chair at the mention of "police," while a middle-aged woman stopped playing with her cell phone and scowled.

Umara fiddled with her *dupatta* self-consciously, wondering why she had chosen today, when she already felt so conspicuous, to take out one of her old *shalwar kameez* suits, instead of wearing pants and an oversized sweater or *kurta*, as she usually did.

"They're not looking to make an arrest? I can't believe Ishaq-*bhai* would be okay with that. I mean, who's to say what this guy might do next? It could be a lot worse than a rock through a window."

The mention of this mysterious Ishaq-*bhai* again made Umara determined to ask where Kashif was spending so much of his time. She knew so little about his friends and acquaintances. And what was all this talk about *maulanas*? Was Nasreen-*bibi* putting ideas into Kashif's head in the effort to make some statement about what a bad mother he had? Then the thought crossed her mind that maybe she was overlooking the obvious. Maybe this was about his father. Was he in touch with him? Did this Ishaq-*bhai* have some connection to Haroon? Why did Kashif mention the police? Was Haroon in some kind of trouble? How dare he get their son involved? Hadn't he done enough damage to this family!

"But if it happened to any other community, it would be a hate crime, wouldn't it!" Kashif said heatedly.

Umara wanted to snatch the phone out of her son's hand, desperate to disentangle herself from the suspicions taking root.

"*Mein ab sab-kuch samajti hun. Apka Abba ke pas jaraha hai!*" she said brusquely, as soon as Kashif hung up.

Kashif looked at his mother incredulously, wondering what on earth she was talking about. He hadn't seen or heard from his father in almost a year. He was about to explain everything when the receptionist called out: "Ms. Siddiqui? Umara Siddiqui?"

Kashif helped his mother to her feet.

"Come this way, please," the receptionist motioned.

Kashif started to walk with his mother, but she waved him down: "*Bhaithiye!*" she ordered harshly. "I go! Myself!"

Kashif obediently released his mother and resumed his seat.

One of the patients had turned up the volume on the television. A reporter standing outside the building housing the mosque where Kashif had spent the better part of the morning appeared on screen. It wasn't even one of the newer buildings that were unmistakably foreign, insofar as they were modelled in the architectural style of a traditional mosque with a dome and minaret. It was just some old office building that had been turned into a place of worship, like the countless Evangelical churches that kept popping up in strip malls and commercial centres—or the kind his parents used to attend when he was a boy.

The patient yawned and was about to change the channel.

"Please leave it!" Kashif intervened.

*...Many volunteers, young and old, have worked tirelessly this morning, painting over the words "Go home" and "No more refugees!" sprayed in red on the mosque's walls. The shards of glass from the broken windows have been cleared away, but it may be harder to calm the shattered nerves of a community still reeling from the effects of what appears to be just the latest in a string of attacks.*

The camera panned across the scene, zooming into the image of windows bandaged up with sheets of plastic and wooden boards. As the camera zoomed back out, a few of the volunteers were caught on camera.

The elderly man peered over his novel to examine Kashif. "You?" he asked, pointing to one of the young males behind the reporter.

Kashif nodded self-consciously, and the man set aside his book to watch the news.

"*We are standing here with Mr. Ishaq Khan, the Director of the Islamic Cultural Centre of Ontario, who has been working with the police since the last such incident: Mr. Khan, how do you think the Muslim community might respond to being targeted again in this manner?"*

"Understandably, not just the Muslim community but also our friends and neighbours from the wider community are quite shaken by this attack. But as Muslims, we are taught to love our neighbours and to work alongside them. In that spirit I would like to say we forgive whoever did this."

"Does that mean you don't wish to press charges in the event of an arrest?"

"We wish for dialogue. We invite whoever did this to let us answer some of the questions and concerns that led them to write that letter and burn the Quran."

"Mr. Khan, is there any other message you would like to send the public today?"

"Only that we extend our deepest gratitude to the entire community for their solidarity and support, especially our young volunteers who came out to help us..."

Umara looked back at her son as she was being chaperoned away. He appeared to be engrossed in the news again.

"*Bilkul Abba ke jaysa hai,*" she muttered, irked once again by the uncanny resemblance between father and son.

"Your son is not with you today?" Doctor Eleniak inquired as Umara entered the office.

"Only me." Umara answered flatly.

Doctor Eleniak waited her for her to take her seat. "The news is not very good, I am afraid, Mrs. Siddiqui."

"Not out of woods?" Umara asked, anxiously rubbing the part of her wrist where the gold bangles she had worn since her wedding had pressed against her skin. She hadn't thought to put them back on since the radiation therapy.

"Unfortunately not. Your body has failed to respond favourably to your last round of treatments."

Umara wasn't sure if she understood correctly. "Failed" seemed to suggest that it was her fault the treatment had not worked. Had she done something wrong? The question made her regret leaving Kashif in the waiting room: "And eating? The tube?"

"Patience and persistence, Ms. Siddiqui."

"How long?" Umara asked again, wondering if her English was to blame or if the doctor just didn't know how to speak plainly.

"Let's just say it will be a while before you're out of those woods."

Umara caught her reflection in the window and touched the side of her face. She thought of the sparrow, comforted that at least she'd had a few crumbs to throw its way before leaving.

# THIRTY-FIVE SECONDS

*F*EBRUARY 12, 2010.
*Bondye bon. May this letter find you protected, sister. Today I write with air in my lungs and a spring in my step. I have received an information package from the group I was telling you about—Canadian Nurses for Haiti. I am going to apply to be among the next group of nurses to help our brothers and sisters. Can you believe it? I may see you again, sooner than we thought.*

Frances put down her sister's letter and rubbed her eyes. She hadn't slept since her arrival. How could one sleep at such a time? The monotonous hum of the computer on the policeman's desk reminded her that the video she had paused—the one she had insisted on watching—was taunting her, behind the black screen. So far she was only able to stomach watching the first twelve seconds. All she could see was a woman walking down a dimly lit street. The woman was wearing a raincoat and a backpack dangled off her shoulder. She used her left hand to hold up a large umbrella. Her right arm swung freely at her side. Frances moved her hand toward the mouse to reactivate the screen and then retracted it. She picked up the letter instead.

*When I think back to when it happened, I could barely breathe with the fear that I had lost you, Frances. The number of days I walked around in a state of shock, not knowing if you were dead or alive, and thinking of the countless others, roofless, homeless, childless, motherless ... the number of nights I woke up with the screams of thousands in my head. Day after day, the news of the horrors worsened to the point that I could not bear to hear another word, or see another image. How it tore me apart not to have any means of contacting you, much less any hope of returning. And the shame that I was too weak to watch the images on a television screen while you were living the horror, the shame that I could hear myself breathe so freely while so many were suffocating under piles of ruin. As God is my witness, Frances, please know that I would have come the moment it happened, but all travel into and out of the country was restricted. Only official and authorized parties, they said.*

Why hadn't Agatha sent her these letters? Frances wondered. The police had recovered them from her backpack. They were stuffed into one envelope. Had she been planning on sending them to her in one batch? Maybe she decided it wasn't worth the bother given the chaotic state of the country's services. Or maybe she was holding on to them for some reason Frances did not as yet understand. None of this made any sense. She read on:

*Someone here told me that even if I could return with the emergency medical teams, I could risk losing my status as a permanent resident. That is what they call the period it takes to become a citizen. I know what it is to complete a nurse's residency, but how strange to complete an immigrant's residency. It is as if I am in training as a citizen! Am I not also a citizen of Haiti? And surely there is much to be learned from a people who lose everything and must rebuild not only their lives, but also their cities and communities, time and time again. But I promise not to dwell on this now, for there is hope that I will be accepted into this program and permitted to return to do God's work—permitted to return to you. I miss you terribly, but just knowing that you are alive and safe gives me hope and strength.* Bondye beni ou. *Agatha.*

Frances put down the letter and looked up at the screen. The image of the woman walking in the rain in the twilight morning hours was emblazoned in her brain, even as some graphic 3D screen-saver swirled about on the monitor. Frances clicked the mouse and the video reappeared, frozen at the image on which she had hit pause. She touched the screen, tracing the outline of the woman. The video camera must have been perched somewhere above, like a bird on a wire, so the people whose images it captured below were faceless. Any chance of seeing the woman's face was further expunged by the large umbrella she was carrying. All one could see were the woman's coat, her swinging arms and legs, and the few metres of pavement surrounding her, which was speckled with leaves. It is autumn, Frances muttered under breath, suddenly struck by the realization that this was her sister's favourite season in this cold northern climate. How much she had raved about it on the rare occasions they had a chance to talk on the phone. She remembered Agatha describing the exhilaration of walking through clouds of falling leaves, walking through a prism of colour—golds, browns, oranges, the darkest greens and crimson, crimson, crimson. But in the monochromatic video the leaves looked like shadows on the pavement, ominous and dark. The leaves on the ground brought to her attention the woman's shoes: a pair of white sneakers. What an excruciatingly long walk it must have been after being on her feet all day long. How cold it must have been at such an hour. And how lonely. If only she hadn't been alone, Frances fumed. Everything would be different now. She wouldn't be sitting in this silent, empty room. She wouldn't be thousands of miles from home. She wouldn't be looking at this ghastly video. She wouldn't be reading these letters. These damn letters!

*August 9, 2010.*
*Bondye bon. May this letter find you protected, sister.*

Her sister's customary greeting jumped out at her from the second letter. Frances looked about in fright. She was still alone in the room where the policewoman had left her, to give her *some space*, they said. This was after she overheard them mention the surveillance camera. When she asked what the camera had to do with anything, they looked at each other uneasily. As they hesitantly informed her of this highly unlikely aspect of the case, her knees buckled for the second or third time that day and she found herself being propped up by several people as they walked her over to a chair. "I must see it," was all she could remember whispering into a policewoman's ear, who sympathetically nodded in agreement. She picked up the letter again.

*I told myself I would not watch another news report about what they are calling the "rescue effort" unless I can be there myself. But a recent setback has made me look back to that terrible day the earth shook its fist, yet again, at our ailing land. Seeing the presidential palace lie in ruin like so many particles of dust, the great cathedral swallowed whole, like Jonah ... even the green rooftops of the hospital where I spent those precious years learning my practice, now lying like so many blades of grass on a carpet of steel pipes, broken tiles, shattered glass, rusty nails, shredded concrete. And below it the people, in their anonymous graves, or the lucky ones among the walking wounded, still unaware, as the injured often are, of the extent of their wounds, the intensity of the pain to come. And all the while I was looking on with one eye closed, hoping against hope that I would not see you lying among the dead. It is too much, Frances. Too much for the eyes to see, for the heart to bear. Please do not misunderstand me: it is not the suffering that I wish to shield myself from. It is the distance between us that sits, more heavily than ever, on my heart today. I was so sure that I had found a way to return. But now this passage has been darkened again. I was just informed that a moratorium has been placed on foreign aid workers. Now even restricted travel is impossible. I don't know why, when there is so much need to this day. But this is what they tell me here. How long this moratorium will last, nobody can tell me. How long before I can return, nobody can say. What good is this life, if it cannot be put to the aid of our Lord? What good is it to look back without being able to move forward? As you can see, my steps are heavy today, but your survival and your well-being help me stay the course.* Bondye beni ou. *Agatha.*

Frances folded the letter, pressing down on the edges as Agatha would have done. If only they could have talked more during these past months, then the space between them would have weighed less heavily upon her. Even though the telecommunications lines had been restored in the richer parts of the city, for most people a telephone was still a luxury, and when one could be borrowed, it was erratic and unstable at best. If only they had talked, then the space ... "to give you some space," she heard the words of the police invade her racing thoughts. The last thing one needed at such a time was space. This was a time for communion. A time for gathering. For companionship and vigil. For eating together, praying together, chanting together, night and day. For bringing together enemy and friend. For making sure the greater journey to come is taken in peace. Frances suddenly felt overcome with anxiety in thinking about the preparations ahead. Everything had to be done the right way, she was going to make sure of that. How many thousands have been robbed of that most basic right, she thought, the image of countless bodies lying on a treeless hillside as fresh in her mind as the image of bulldozers tearing up an already wounded land for their unmarked graves. She was about to get up and call the policewoman—the kind one who had shown so much compassion—to beg her to let her take her sister home, to beg her to let her take her home now, without further delay, while there was still time to do things right. Then the image on the screen caught her eye. She noticed she had hit pause at fifteen seconds rather than twelve seconds, and there was the shadow—a half shadow, like half a man — frozen at the far right edge of the screen. She braced herself and was about to hit play when an icy chill gripped her entire body and her hand froze, like the image on the screen. She hugged herself, rubbing her hands on the sides of her arms to warm herself up. Then she picked up the next letter, desperate to hear her sister's voice.

*September 30, 2010.*
*Bondye bon. May this letter find you protected, sister. I cannot explain in words the state of my heart today so I will just speak plainly. My application has been rejected. I had to read the letter at least three times to understand the reason. Before I tell you what it is, I have to be honest with you. Yes, it is time for confession. Life has not turned out as I planned here. Forgive me for burdening you with this—I am ashamed to share such thoughts with you, when you have seen so much, endured so much. This is not your weight to bear. It is mine and mine alone. But you need to know. I need to tell you the truth about my situation.*

Frances stopped reading. Surely she had endured enough aftershocks for one lifetime. Whatever her sister had to confess, she did not want to know. Putting the letters aside, she reactivated the video at fifteen seconds, where she had hit pause, partly to prevent herself from finishing the letter and partly because she knew she would not be able to leave the room till she watched the video in its entirety. She owed her sister that much. She regretted her decision as soon as the image of the man reappeared, his menacing shadow preceding him. Even at the angle the camera had recorded his movement, she could see he was tall and burly. Seeing him walking like that—just steps away, seconds away—made her sick to her stomach. She covered her mouth and hit pause again. She looked at the screen, her hand still over her mouth, unsure whether it was the nausea she was trying to suppress or the sound of her dread. The image was freeze-framed at a point where the man put his hand under an opening in his jacket, as if he were reaching for something inside it. It couldn't be, she thought. Had he been reaching for the knife? She hit play again with a trembling hand, determined to have the courage to witness what the camera had witnessed, determined to have the courage to face this monster as he had been faced. With great courage, the police had told her. She was a brave woman, the words reverberated in her mind as he came to view again, his head concealed by a baseball hat. She noticed that only seconds after the camera caught his image, he hastened his steps. Was it at that moment he had decided to attack her? Had he planned it all along? But why? she agonized. What caused such rage against a poor, helpless woman, whose only desire was to get home and rest her tired feet after a long day's work? Why? she had pleaded to the police for answers. But they had none. None that could satisfy her. He didn't rob her. Her wallet and its contents looked as if they hadn't been touched. The suspect in custody was neither a known felon nor a civilian with any record of a violent history. In fact, he was a boy—fifteen or sixteen—and would be convicted as a minor. She couldn't believe it. He didn't look like some helpless child, she thought, enraged. He looked determined, like a bird hunting its prey. But why? Why would a boy want to attack a stranger? Maybe they weren't strangers, she surmised. Were they going to investigate this further? Maybe he was obsessed with her. Stalking her. Or maybe it was what they called a hate crime. That was not out of the realm of possibility, was it? No, this was highly unlikely, they were quick to assure her. He had confessed to everything upon his arrest but had not shown any indication of knowing his victim, much less her race. In fact, the crime scene was littered with his DNA. The sign of an amateur, they had remarked—maybe even a first time offender. There's been an eruption of teenage violence recently, they noted when she looked at them disbelievingly. It seemed likely that this incident, too, was of that nature. They were sorry, so very sorry, they couldn't tell her more. An incident? How could there be any justice for an incident? she had wanted to scream. Surely something so brutal and so senseless deserved further investigation? She picked up the letter again, desperate for answers, desperate to make sense of it all. Maybe the letters contained a clue that the police had missed. Something that would prove this was more than an incident. More than some indiscriminate act of violence. More than some random event. The terrible outcome would be the same but at least there would be an explanation. Frances picked up the letter again, retracing the place where she had stopped reading a few minutes earlier.

*The truth is I am one of the fortunate ones, because I have "a foot in the door"*—un pied dans la place! *These local expressions are strange, aren't they? A foot in the door seems like a painful and humiliating predicament. Does it mean the door has been closed on you? Or that you have pushed your way through the door, like an unwanted guest?*

Frances had to pause again. She and Agatha always responded to things in such similar ways, so much so that they had been teased all their lives about being twins. Of course they weren't twins. They were born several years apart, and Agatha was the younger of the two but everyone thought of her as the older one. She was always so strong. She had always been her protector.

*Sister, I know I am talking in circles. It's just that I find this so hard to admit. The truth is that I have not been working as a nurse. I work at the hospital* — *that much is true. And if you call changing bedpans, bathing the invalid, or pushing wheelchairs across hallways being a nurse, then perhaps.... But on days like today I am filled with regret. Regret that I had not stayed where I was needed. Among people who would not have asked me to fetch the "real nurse" or pushed me out of the way when a patient is in distress. Here I am changing urine-stained sheets when I should be changing bandages; here I am what they call an "auxiliary"—a helping hand. Sometimes even less, where there are almost one hundred nurses per patient and yet they complain of a nursing shortage. And to think I have left behind a land where our healers lay dying alongside their patients, and our hospitals and schools lie in rubble below them. I know there are some of the world's best medical teams there right now. But their task is to patch up the broken pieces and leave. Who is there for the long-haul? Three years, our President said—it will take at least three years just to clean up the city. What about the people? How long will it take to tend to their wounds? How many generations? I know, I know. I am talking in circles again. The fact is, up until this point I had hope that they would take my application seriously, that they would see how ready I am to face whatever awaits us in the place I know better than anyone here. Up until today, that is, when I received this dreadful letter, saying I am not qualified to be part of their volunteer medical assistance unit. While they appreciate my training, they say, the applicant must be a registered nurse in Canada. As this is not my case, and in light of my training in Haiti, I am being encouraged to re-apply under the general program, as part of a civilian volunteer effort, which may be needed in the years to come. So that is that, Frances. They call me a civilian. I call myself a fraud. What else can I be if I am not the nurse I claim to be? Never more acutely have I felt the admonition, in the Book of James: What good is it, my brothers and sisters, if someone claims to have faith but has no deeds? Can such faith save them?*

*In the same way, faith by itself, if not accompanied by action, is dead.... I hope you can find it in your heart to forgive me, my sister, for my grievous inaction.* Bondye beni ou. *Agatha.*

Forgive you! Frances fumed. How can I forgive you! All this time Frances had consoled herself that Agatha was far from the chaos—from the war zone their city had become. Thousands still lived in the streets in makeshift shelters made out of anything they could find—cardboard, a broken car door, sheet metal, strips of cloth—since any building that hadn't collapsed was being used to house the wounded, the invalid, the dying. The one thing that gave her solace was that at least she didn't have to worry about Agatha. Agatha was safe, living the life she had worked so hard to make for herself. *Woch nan dlo pa konnen doulè wòch nan solèy*, Frances found herself reciting the old proverb: *The rock in the water does not know the pain of the rock in the sun.* How foolish she had been, not thinking for a minute of her sister's struggles, her sister's pain. And to think that it was *she* who talked Agatha into leaving! She had pushed and pushed for months, trying to convince her it was the right thing to do—that if she had the chance, then she should take it. Why had she insisted so much? Frances admonished herself. None of the reasons seemed clear to her anymore. Had their situation been so desperate? At least back home Agatha worked as a nurse. But together they were barely ekeing out a living. So many like them got by just on the little money families sent them from abroad. Agatha didn't want to go without her—this she remembered clearly. But there was no chance of their going together. Oh, why did she push her to go? Why couldn't she leave well enough alone? If anyone needed to beg forgiveness ... *Si mwen menm ki ta dwe mande padon.* Forgive me, Frances gasped through her tears. Unable to read another word, she started to gather the letters together. She would finish reading them at another time, a time when it did not hurt so much. Then she noticed the date at the top of the page of the one letter she had not as yet read: October 21. Almost nine days ago, she thought, and urgently pulled it out from the bundle. As soon as she unfolded the paper, the jasmine perfume Agatha loved permeated the room. Frances held the letter away from her, wanting to preserve her sister's scent, not wanting to stain it with her tears.

*October 21, 2010*
*Bondye bon. In his heart a man plans his course, but the Lord determines his steps. Today I keep my letter short, dear Frances, because my steps have been determined, and I walk with joy and purpose once again. I must confess that in the months following the earthquake I wrote many letters to you but I could not get myself to send them. How could I burden you with my regrets and petty disappointments at such a time? Nor did I think they would reach you even if I had. But now you must hear what I have to say. In fact, if I could, I would go to the Cross that sits atop the pretty mountain-park at the centre of this city, and I would shout out my news for all to hear. (You should know that the Cross was erected centuries ago by the city's founder when the city was destroyed by a disastrous flood. I only know this because I once walked to the top of the mountain to see the Cross for myself. It was my private little pilgrimage to give thanks for my arrival.) So imagine that I am saying this from the city's highest summit, the one that is closest to Our Father, when you read this: I am coming home!*

*Home!* The word struck her like a final blow, loosening her grip on the letter. Frances looked around the room, thinking that someone had entered. There was no one there. She held down the letter on the table and traced the words on the page, all the force of her energy directed toward them: *I am coming home.* The phrase assaulted her like the carnage of a fallen city, making it hard to think, hard to move, hard to breathe. It was too much. Too much. In the next second the heaviness was replaced with guilt. Guilt for not feeling the joy these words so clearly conveyed for her sister. She clicked the mouse and reactivated the screen, compelled to watch the video again, but this time from beginning to end—all thirty-five seconds. She watched the woman walking in the lonely hours of the early morning, well before others had risen. Only unlike them she had already finished a long day's work. All she wanted was to go home and rest her feet, to catch a few hours of sleep, to gather strength so she could start all over again, the next day. The next day. She should have had a next day, Frances raged inwardly. And then the man—no, the boy, as the police had corrected her—reappeared again, walking only steps behind her. He must have been waiting in the shadows. He put his hand in his jacket. It must have been to pull out the knife—a kitchen knife, the police had told her. He is just a boy, she heard the words again. Was that his mother's knife? The one she used to prepare his dinners? She remembered wanting to ask the police this question, but the details assaulted her in spliced images and sounds, and she could not be sure if any of it was real. But his shadow was real, wasn't it? He was real when he followed her, hastening his steps till he was out of the frame. It was impossible to imagine it and yet here it was, for all to see, on a street video surveillance camera. But what about the things that were not seen? The things beyond the camera's frame? Like the nine stab wounds to her arms, her back, her chest, and her left leg? Like the fact that she was dead before the paramedics arrived because of one fatal wound. Which one, she asked, preparing herself for information whose delivery by a middle-aged policeman—his hat tilted on a crop of blond hair, his eyes expressionless and cool, his burly stature incongruous against a light so soft it gave him an absurdly ethereal quality, like a halo—she knew would stay with her forever. Which one, she asked again, refusing to be spared a single detail. The one to the upper left part of the abdomen—to the spleen, he qualified. She was a nurse, she recalled saying softly, more to herself than to the policeman. She would have known in that instant. She would have known where he had stabbed her. She would have known what that meant. She would have known that it would be a matter of hours before she bled out. That there would be no hope of survival. She would have known. She would have known. She would have known. Frances put her head in her hands and sobbed inconsolably for the first time since her arrival. She cried and cried and cried, unaware that the kind policewoman had come into the room and was touching her arm, telling her it was time to go. Time to face whatever else needed to be faced. She lifted her head up and saw the letter still open on the table, the words blurry through her cloud of tears. She had to finish reading it, she told herself. She owed her sister that much. She owed her sister that and so much more. She picked up the letter and looked at the policewoman who seemed to understand what she needed, leaving the room as unobtrusively as she had entered, leaving Frances alone with her sister's letters.

*I am coming home because, finally, I have completed my status as a permanent resident. Do you know what this means, Frances? This means that I can come and go as I please! I can travel like any Canadian citizen. Free to leave, free to return, as I please. But return to what? I have given this so much thought in the past few months. I have wondered if I will ever have a claim on this land. And no matter what I do, will it ever really wish to claim me? It won't be long before I take the citizen's oath, but what about the oath I took as a nurse? And, most importantly, what about my oath to you, that your sacrifices would not be in vain? It is to you I owe the biggest debt, Frances. If it weren't for you and all those years you worked so hard to pay for my training.... How much you suffered in that dreadful place, cutting and sewing, cutting and sewing, all day long. And how we would joke and say that I, too, was learning to cut and to sew just so I could patch you up every time you came home, your hands bleeding from the pokes and pricks of those industrial machines. What a terrible joke to make, Frances! But we laughed all the same. What was there to do but laugh? But in all seriousness, now, I read somewhere that even those factories have shut down, and I wonder how you are surviving? You haven't been entirely honest with me either, have you? All of your assurances that you are managing just fine, that I have nothing to be concerned about—these you say to protect me. And all I can do is hope that the few money transfers I have made in the last months have reached you, but with the state of our banks I cannot even be certain of this. And now there are even fewer and fewer updates about what is going on since the world's attention has been diverted by other events as spectacular as our own. The foreign aid has dried up and the emergency teams have packed up and gone but what lies ahead for us? Years of rebuilding, years of finding our way again, our city broken, like our hearts. What lies ahead but healing? So, you see, there is nothing else for me to do here, a place where all I can do is pray. At least in these past few months I have been forced to remain idle, in this state of limbo, I have found comfort in the saying: You can do more than pray after you've prayed, but you cannot do more than pray until you have prayed. It is time now to do more than pray. It is time to come home.* Bondye nou an Fidel. *Agatha.*

Frances wanted desperately to answer Agatha's questions, to allay her fears, to tell her that she had received the money she had sent—money without which she would not have been able to make this long journey for the woman in the path of a random event who fought, till the very last second, to live—just enough, that is, to take her sister home.

# CROSSING OVER

"KRISHNA, YOU'RE driving too fast! The roads are a skating rink as it is!" Radha squealed, checking for the hundredth time if her seatbelt was securely fastened.

"I know how icy it is out there!" Krishna sputtered, speeding up an extra five kilometres.

"If we had only looked at the weather channel before leaving, I would have cancelled our dinner with the Akbars."

"Not that I would have minded skipping this dinner, but you don't think I was aware it was snowing? Didn't you see me out there with the snow-blower before leaving? Who do you think cleared the driveway?" Krishna rejoindered, his blood pressure rising with the speedometer. He could feel the car begin to skid so he gently pumped his brakes, just as he had been shown at Driver's Ed all those years back. New immigrants had to learn to drive again, apparently. And he was grateful for it too, because navigating one's way past bullock carts, rickshaws, potholes, and an onslaught of pedestrians on a Mumbai boulevard now seemed like a walk-in-the-park. In a coastal Atlantic city like Halifax, an average drive on a winter's day involved bypassing a twenty-ton snow plough, braking for deer to avoid charges of fauna-manslaughter, while hitting a patch of black ice just as one's wiper blades gave out and left you blind in the middle of a blizzard on a dim-lit winding road. He had learned early on that acute dexterity, bionic peripheral vision, and nerves of steel were the basics of road preparedness here.

A quarter of a century in this country and we've never so much as swerved off the road, but she still doesn't trust my winter driving, he thought irritably. Besides, Radha drove at a steady forty-eight kilometres per hour, sun or snow, rain or shine, so he wasn't about to take driving tips from her. And now that he fancied himself a road-hardy Canadian driver in what he liked to call "our true north," an anthemic phrase that had stuck in his brain like a Vedic mantra since their citizenship ceremony, he was hard pressed to fuss over a few patches of ice and a humdrum snowstorm. This province alone spends five million in tax payers' dollars just to salt the roads each winter; they have handsomely paid civil servants working around the clock to keep our streets safe while people like Radha get their beauty sleep; they have a system here—structure, order.

It's a small price to pay for civilization, Krishna reasoned as he over-shot the Akbars' driveway and parked at the edge of the front lawn, which was buried under several feet of snow.

"Houston: the Eagle has landed!" he proclaimed theatrically, pushing the ignition button and bailing himself out of the car as purposefully as Buzz Aldrin. As he trudged up what he assessed to be nothing less than a treacherous moon-walk on Tariq Akbar's poorly shovelled driveway, he realized that his wife was nowhere in sight. Blast it, where the devil is that woman now? A final lipstick touch-up? It's only the Akbars!

Radha was still holed up in the car. Seeing her wrapping her knuckles on the window, Krishna let out an affectionate chortle, mumbled something under his breath, and used the indents created by his heavy winter boots in the freshly fallen snow to retrace his steps back down the driveway.

Radha sat with her arms crossed as she watched her husband rummage through just about every pocket of his winter coat for something or other. Then he pulled off one glove and set off on a second pocket-rummaging expedition till he fished out a small cylinder.

"Always prepared!" he barked triumphantly, holding up a lock de-icer for Radha's admiration.

Radha was neither amused nor impressed as she watched her husband fumble with the de-icer in the slow, mechanical gestures she had come to identify as uniquely his.

"It isn't working!" Krishna yelled, as he tried to pry his hand off the ice-encrusted passenger door handle.

"What?" Radha yelled back.

"The door's still frozen shut! ... Look, you will have to cross over the gear stick and get out from the driver's side!"

"The driver? You're the driver!"

"No! The driver's *side!*" Krishna said again. Then, miming the shape of a bridge and speaking slowly: "*Cross over* to the *driver's side!*"

"Cross over?"

"Yes!"

"No!"

"Why ever not?" Krishna's patience was waning, his eyelashes weighed down with snowflakes.

"I cannot!" Radha repeated, drawing out the "not" for added emphasis. She had spent an uncharacteristic amount of time pleating her sari tonight. For some reason it was not cooperating. Maybe it was sticking because of the static from the woollen stockings she had worn. Or maybe it was because they hadn't seen Mumtaz and Tariq in a while and the invitation was making her anxious. Or maybe it was just one of those days. And now she was stuck in the car without a winter coat! All she had for warmth was a grey cashmere shawl, stockings, and leather gloves. Nor had she worn her thermal boots since she had fully expected having to walk no more than a few steps, from the car to the Akbars' doorstep, supported by the extended arm of a gentleman.

"What do you mean you 'cannot'?" her husband hollered.

"I'm wearing a sari! You know I can't cross over like this! Just open my door!"

Krishna squirted a generous amount of de-icer into the passenger door lock again, but to no avail. He was beginning to feel the cold creep into his extremities.

"Will you please cross over, sari or no sari! I can't open the door!"

"I'm telling you I cannot!"

"Then, what do you want me to do? Break the door down?"

"Break it if you have to!" Radha retorted imperiously. "But I will *not* cross over!"

Realizing his wife would have sat in the car all night if only for her unfaltering sense of propriety—a quality whose utility he now questioned—Krishna knew he didn't stand a chance. She would rather freeze to death than hike up her sari, of this there was no doubt in his mind. "That's it, then! I'm going in! Let me know when you decide to show a little common sense."

"Krishna!" Radha yelped like a puppy left behind in its owner's car at a grocery store parking lot.

Of course, Krishna had no intention of leaving his wife in the car. Of course, he was going to ask Tariq for help. But to say he wasn't bothered by the fact that, after all these years and all these winters, she still refused to wear more sensible clothing would be a lie. Tradition had its time and place and a snow-covered land in sub-zero temperatures in the middle of the night was neither the time nor the place. Why couldn't she be more like Tariq's wife, Mumtaz, who adopted western attire with little fuss, and who happened to look quite fetching in those pantsuits of hers, he reflected rather sheepishly.

"*As-Salam Alaikum*, Krishna!" Tariq Akbar exclaimed as he opened a pine-scented, Christmas-wreathed front door.

"*Namaste*," Krishna replied distractedly.

Tariq was instantly unnerved. Would it kill him to say "*W'Alaikum Salam*"? It was *his* house, after all. He was owed a modicum of respect! Tariq thought indignantly, fully preparing himself for an unpleasant evening. Why had he conceded to playing the gracious host tonight? Mumtaz had pushed for the dinner, even though she knew how much Krishna and his wife—in fact, even more so his wife—got under his skin. He perked up when he noticed she wasn't there. "Where's Radha? Not feeling well?"

"She's here! She's just stuck in the car! Her door's locked and she refuses to cross over to the driver's seat because she's afraid of getting her precious sari unravelled. Her husband's brains she doesn't worry about unravelling, but her sari ... God forbid! I don't know what else she wants me to do. Smash the lock with a tire-iron or something? It's a Mercedez! That's a ten-thousand dollar door!"

Tariq winced over Krishna's irksome habit of reminding him how much money he made. First, their waterfront property on the Bedford Harbour, then their daughter's exorbitant wedding, and now this latest indulgence. Who did he think he was kidding, driving around in a hundred-thousand dollar car? They both came from a time and a place where only sheikhs and princes drove cars like that.

"I'm sure we'll find another way," he said, trying his utmost to maintain his cool while hurriedly ushering Krishna inside the house so as not to waste the heating. He had become acutely conscious of the hefty price of running a household in a cold climate. Even keeping the fireplace going barely cut down on costs. He couldn't get over how exorbitant the price of firewood was—almost the equivalent of a monthly gas bill. He continually griped about the fact that they were surrounded by forest as far as the eye could see, and yet they paid through their noses for wood. This would lead him to the related pet peeve that no one had figured out how to harness all this natural energy, an observation that was generally punctuated with the taunt: And they call *this* the *developed* world!

Radha watched the Akbars' front door close as she sat helpless in the car. Both her husband and Tariq had abandoned her. So typical, she bemoaned. First these men talk us into coming to this arctic outpost, and then they leave it up to us to figure out how to survive!

Snow brought in by a gust of north-westerly winds started to blanket the driver's side of the car, making Radha feel boxed in, much as she had felt in those early years as a new immigrant. How odd that she had never felt like this in Mumbai, she mused, not even while she was taking time off work to raise their newborn son. If their home was not always bustling with friends and family, there were so many occasions and events to get her out of the house. But even though she loved that precious time with her son, she had been eager to get back to work. There was a shortage of teachers at the time and the school board had set a new rising pay scale commensurate with one's level of education. This would mean a considerable increase in salary for someone like her—someone with a graduate degree. If only she had known then what she knew now, she may have worked harder to convince Krishna not to emigrate.

But Krishna had been so determined, and all of his arguments appeared perfectly sound at the time: they had a points system there, he said; they had a better chance than anyone of being successful applicants because of their skills and their education; and all the benefits of working in the West would pay off in spades for their children. When he felt her yielding to the idea, he dared to add: and what about the adventure of it all? Of course, they wouldn't be pioneers because others had made the journey long before them. But putting down roots in a country that had only recently opened its doors to people like them, looking to build its national character in new and exciting ways, would be a welcome relief from a place mired in thousands of years of squabbles and rivalries. He even boasted about how they were all former British imperial subjects and thus part of the same historical lineage. She had wanted to remind him of that nasty *Komagata Maru* affair, but held back. Theirs was a young marriage and she had to admit that she got caught up in the romance of it all: a husband and wife and their first-born child leaving everything and everyone behind to make a new life for themselves in such an exotic and distant land.

Acquaintances and neighbours would often ask them why they immigrated to Canada, fully expecting a heart-wrenching sob story. They must have been escaping something terrible? Poverty, war, oppression? True, they would never be wealthy back home but, in every way that counted, their life in the world they left behind was a good one. It was hard to explain this thirst that her husband had for adventure, which she could only attribute to his own sense of the sublime. Radha was likely partly to blame for all that poetry she used to read to him in the early days of their marriage. How enamoured he was by her ability to recite, verbatim, some of her favourite works by Shelley, Bryon, and Blake. He would get so caught up in their otherworldly visions. Was it any wonder he fancied himself something of a modern-day Magellan?

Radha noticed her window frosting over in fractal-like patterns. If Krishna didn't get back soon, she would be entombed in a crypt of unforgiving whiteness. She took a deep breath in and exhaled through her mouth, a breathing exercise her yogi insisted she perform whenever she felt anxious, which was more often than not. She looked through the empty spaces between the frosted glass and remarked how quiet the street was. Sitting in the car on a dark street reminded her of one her favourite poems, but she had to scour her brain to remember the words. It had been so long since she had been in front of the classroom that her repertoire of poems had long since slipped out of her memory. There was something about a rock, she thought. A rock and a chain. It killed her not to remember. She tried again, this time trying to excise the useless information—the banalities of her daily "to do" list—that generally cluttered her mind these days. How could she have forgotten? So what if she wasn't a teacher anymore? It wasn't so very long ago when all this knowledge was as essential to her as breathing.

She peered out of the window again and realized that someone was waving to her from inside the house. She squinted and strained to see beyond the snowfall. It was Mumtaz. She waved back half-heartedly, certain that Mumtaz wouldn't be able to see her, but reassured that at least they all hadn't forgotten about her.

Even through the veil of frost, ice, and blowing snow, Mumtaz cut such an elegant figure, Radha thought. Not only was she a beautiful woman, but she managed to carry herself with a grace and confidence that Radha could never emulate. But more than any of these attributes, Mumtaz fit in here in a way that she didn't or couldn't. For one, she spoke English like a British aristocrat, no doubt from all the years she and Tariq had spent abroad, hobnobbing in cosmopolitan circles. Radha felt that Mumtaz laid on the accent a bit thick, but her elongated "a's" and her staccato "t's" seemed worth the price of any number of professional credentials. The fact of the matter was that Mumtaz was out there, working and earning a living, while she was cooped up at home with little to do but volunteer at the South Asian women's association or plan the occasional dinner party. It was ironic really: Mumtaz was the uneducated one but managed to come across as worldly and employable; Radha was the educated one and managed to come across as "not meeting the standards."

This made Radha's discovery of what she privately referred to as Mumtaz's "second migration"—not from country-to-country but from home-to-world—as unsettling as it was unsurprising. She was nonetheless speechless the day she found Mumtaz working at the Tea Store.

\*\*\*

"Radha! How marvelous to see you! What brings you out on such a tempestuous day!"

"Oh, I was going a little stir crazy at home! You too, I see," Radha said presumptuously.

"Right. Well, I…"

Just then they were interrupted by a younger woman who called out: "Taz, we need someone on cash."

Mumtaz woodenly walked over to the cash register to ring in a customer's purchase. Radha was left staring blankly at a shelf of teapots, dumbfounded by this highly unexpected turn of events. Since when did Mumtaz work? The Akbars, unlike them, had come here on an entrepreneurial visa. They lived quite lavishly. They were people who had wined and dined ambassadors and celebrities. In their house, one sat on bone-inlaid furniture, dined with soft lighting emanating from hanging *fanooses*, gazed into Venetian mirrors, and walked on Oriental rugs which, as Mumtaz once informed her, were heirlooms from Isphahan and Balochistan, while the men extinguished their cigarettes in ashtrays chiselled out of Himalayan slopes or finely etched brass. And it was all the real deal: purchased on site and carted across continents in well-insured shipping containers; everything in that house was authentic and authenticated, rather than the kind of Chinese imitations Radha liked to buy at the big-box stores. She and Krishna always felt a bit out of sorts at the Akbar home, even now, considering theirs was a much more humble beginning. They had used up all their savings in the application process to Canada, coming to the country with a screaming baby and a few suitcases filled with nothing but the value of their respective degrees in education and accounting.

If truth be told, Radha had reflected on more than one occasion, their friendship with the Akbars was born out of chance and necessity. If Krishna had not dealt with Tariq the day he came to the bank to apply for a mortgage, they would never have met. Had she and Krishna had their own circle of friends back then, they would likely never have asked the Akbars, who were new arrivals at the time, for dinner. The community was so small in those early days. It was a relief to meet the Akbars, whose pre-partition roots in India were reason enough to lay the groundwork for a friendship in a sleepy

Maritime town, thousands of miles from the Subcontinent.

Still, this did not take away from the fact that theirs was a friendship that was continually tested by their obvious differences, including their husbands' common impulse to always be right. If history, politics, and religion weren't the basis of Tariq's and Krishna's perpetual sparring, then their vastly different trajectories to the West filled the space between them with epic tension, Krishna looking on their migration with unqualified pride and Tariq looking on his with unqualified resentment.

Perhaps the increasing gulf between them was an unfortunate but natural evolution of their friendship, Radha surmised. Come to think of it, the gulf had only widened since that day at the Tea Store.

Mumtaz walked back to Radha who nervously fidgeted with a glass tea pot, oddly shaped like a pagoda. "Can I help you find something special today?" she asked officiously.

"Special?"

"Yes, in fact we have a stupendous special this week: buy one of our newest tea blends and get a second one for fifty percent off!"

"Oh no … I was just … browsing."

Mumtaz seemed distracted, another customer demanding her attention at the cash register, so she excused herself again before Radha had a chance to escape. This time she was close enough to hear Mumtaz chatting to the other sales clerk while ringing in the customer's purchase.

"Oh, darling, you really mustn't settle! You're far too dear a catch to accept some tawdry affair!" The two of them twittered and chuckled like they were bosom buddies, the vast differences in age and background seeming far too little a thing to stand between Mumtaz and this new world she seemed to inhabit like a second skin. It was enough to bring Radha to the brink of an anxiety attack, but she managed to walk over to the cash register, mumble a flustered goodbye, and leave without further ado.

Neither had spoken to each other for months before Mumtaz encountered Radha at the mall again. This time she was on a lunch break, and asked Radha if she would join her. Radha could see no way out of the invitation. She prepared herself for an awkward conversation, but Mumtaz seemed in genuine need of a sympathetic ear. They had fallen on such hard times that even their home was at risk of foreclosure, Mumtaz said, disburdening herself almost the moment they sat down in the food court. When Radha inquired into what she euphemistically referred to as Tariq's "situation," Mumtaz explained that her husband had proved to be unemployable. Apparently, she remarked with uncharacteristic cynicism, his money was good enough to secure them immigration papers, but the lifetime of business acumen he brought with him wasn't worth so much as the price of the Customs declaration form. He had even gone so far as to apply for a taxi licence, but that didn't pan out because of his ailing health. On this note, Mumtaz was surprisingly frank, admitting that her husband had sunk into a depression but refused to seek any kind of clinical treatment or professional help.

This finally pushed Mumtaz to take action and find work, anywhere she could get it. She had always helped Tariq with whatever urgent matters his business demanded, but she had never been "out there" in the regular workforce, and she certainly had no expectation that she could succeed in getting a job—any kind of job—where her husband had failed. As luck would have it, she said, suddenly sitting tall in her seat, she was window shopping at the mall one day when she saw a Help Wanted sign for a sales clerk at the new Tea Store, so she just *went for it*.

"You know how I can't get through the day without at least six cups of tea!" she winked lightheartedly. "So I thought if anyone could sell tea, I could. Besides, we change so much of ourselves to fit in here but our *chai*—I'll be damned if our *chai* is going to become Canadian too. Don't they know how silly it is to say '*chai* tea,' as if *chai* is an English word, when all they are really saying is "tea tea!"

Radha smiled weakly. She, too, was irritated by *chai* being packaged and consumed as if it were some kind of North American invention, but she knew Mumtaz was just trying to put a positive spin on the situation—just trying to make lemonade out of lemons, or *chai* out of spoiled milk.

"And now I get to set the record straight about tea being a South Asian drink that the British took from us, not the other way around!" Mumtaz continued, seemingly determined to turn her attention to lighter subjects now that her confession was over.

As she prattled on about the different kinds of tea they sold at the store for ridiculous prices, Radha found herself preoccupied by her own "situation"—perhaps one of the few things she and Tariq had in common, she reflected in hindsight. In fact, she desperately wanted to make some confessions of her own, such as how mortified she was that day at the store, not because she was embarrassed for her friend, but because Mumtaz had attained, against all odds, what she was unable to attain with all of her training and education. But something kept her from sharing her personal struggle with her friend. Maybe it was because she was a little jealous of Mumtaz who, with no apparent skill set and no qualifications, had ventured out into this impenetrable job market without running into a hundred walls. Or maybe she was resentful of Mumtaz who had the advantage of her good looks and fair complexion. Someone for whom words like "darling," "tawdry," and "stupendous" rolled off her tongue like melted *ghee*; someone who wore pants and sweaters, not saris and *bindis*, and who just seemed to belong, no matter where she was or what she did.

I, too, just *went for it*, didn't I? Radha reflected bitterly. She had put herself out there many, many times, she wanted to tell Mumtaz, but this was a source of private humiliation that she was unable to share with anyone, even Krishna. How many jobs had she applied for with the same results: "Of course, we can see you have plenty of experience, Mrs. Chatterjee, but rules are rules," countless Human Resources directors had told her at countless schools. Her self-esteem took a special kind of beating when she was matter-of-factly asked why she was applying to be an English teacher when English was not her native language. "There are certain standards we have to maintain," the director had added, not so much as giving her a chance to respond that English was as much a first language to her as Hindi, and that he would do well to remember his own British imperial history. "You understand, of course...."

Yes, she understood. She understood perfectly. She understood that a woman in a *sari*, a long black plait and a red dot on her forehead was not qualified enough to relate to a room full of North American teenagers. She understood that an English teacher had to walk and talk a certain way to teach Shakespeare and Blake, and she neither talked the talk nor walked the walk. She understood that in this country her qualifications were no better than a weight around a drowning man's neck.

Still, her determination held sway over the humiliation she had suffered, at least for time enough to endure a few more meetings with school board officials, meetings for which she shed the *bindi* and sari and wore suits, albeit a little ill-fitting. She even took pronunciation classes at a community college, as she had been advised by some workshop counsellor at the Ministry, but she still couldn't land an interview, not even as a substitute teacher. Instead, she was told to "upgrade" her skills, to consider an internship, to take job-search workshops, even to return to university to get an additional degree, despite the fact that she held degrees in English *and* Education.

\*\*\*

Radha looked up at the house again, but the car was almost completely blanketed in snow and the window pane was covered in frost. She managed to scrape a portion of the window clean from the inside and look out but all she could see was a haze of lights emanating from the house. Everything else was a sea of black speckled by fuzzy white dots, like an old television monitor with no signal.

How quiet everything is here, she remarked again. How still. Such empty spaces. Such giant skies. Such a contrast to everything she had known. Her land, her weather, her sky. And then she remembered, the words sliding off her tongue as effortlessly as Mumtaz's colourful vocabulary:

*A silent suffering and intense,*
*The rock, the vulture, and the chain*
*All that the proud can feel of pain,*
*The agony they do not show,*
*The suffocating sense of woe*
*Which speaks but in its loneliness.*
*And then is jealous lest the sky*
*Should have a listener, nor will sigh*
*Until its voice is echoless.*

"Until its voice is echoless," she repeated to herself, when she noticed that the moisture from her breath had cleared a portion of the frosted pane just long enough for her to see if Mumtaz was still looking out at her from the living room window.

She wondered how the Akbars were managing to stay afloat on Mumtaz's meagre wages. It had been years since that encounter at the mall. It was true that they had not seen each other much, at least not socially, for a good long while, the dinner invitations to each of their homes growing less frequent. Perhaps the bond that had sealed their friendship in the early days was no longer enough to hold them together, not only because of each family's changing circumstances, but also because the world around them was changing so rapidly. The city itself, like the people in it, had changed dramatically. The Maritime provinces' drive to make the region a more attractive destination for new immigrants, opening up business opportunities in the oil exploration and renewable energy sectors, had brought in a new wave of wealthy investors from the Middle East and elsewhere. These were desirable contacts that Krishna, as the bank's Chief Financial Officer, could cultivate with hefty investment incentives, and Radha felt obliged to host with lavish dinner parties, a joint effort that had widened their social circle and social standing in leaps and bounds.

She had been meaning to invite them to one of their last soirées, but had just assumed that Mumtaz would neither have the energy nor the time. Now she felt a little guilty for allowing it to get to the point that a dinner invitation had to come from the Akbars.

She assumed Mumtaz was dreading this dinner as much as she was, speculating that the invitation was likely Tariq's idea for whatever agenda he might have had to get an audience with Krishna. She could not imagine his wanting to be social for any other reason. Probably, he would have pushed for it sooner had it not been for their "situation," which Tariq undoubtedly preferred to keep under the radar though, again, she had to own up to the fact that his instinct for self-protection was one she shared. Yet, she had also seen enough of Tariq's temperament to know that "the situation" must have been taking its toll on them, on their marriage, in all kinds of insidious ways. For one, the idea of his wife supporting the family must have been killing him. If anything, his depression must have worsened. To be fair though, she allowed herself to admit, such a thing would likely be the death of Krishna too. After all, what if things had been reversed for them? What if she were the one to find work as a teacher and he wasn't able to secure a position in his field? What then?

Radha thought of her brief chat over the phone with Mumtaz earlier that week, when she had called out of the blue to invite them to dinner. Hadn't she said something about accepting a managerial position at one of the Tea Store's new outlets? Maybe this was a celebratory dinner, though she couldn't imagine Mumtaz making a show of such a thing, even at the best of times.

She wondered why she had been so quick to assume that Mumtaz was just in survival mode. Maybe the work meant far more to her than a paycheque, after all. Had she not taken great pride in the fact that she had the highest sales record in the province? And why had she diminished Mumtaz's work as the kind of "survival job" any immigrant could get? Was it because she assumed that only the kind of work that demanded credentials and qualifications was hard to come by? She had read that even retail jobs were few and far between these days. After everything she had gone through to find work in years past, Radha wasn't convinced that she'd be any more employable as a store clerk than as a teacher—or anything else, for that matter.

Thinking back on their first encounter at the Tea Store again, Radha realized that Mumtaz had looked anything but miserable in her job that day—she was thriving, laughing, and talking to co-workers and customers alike. Was it because she was discovering a new side of herself and her talents, or was it because she was away from the doom and gloom that Tariq must have cast over the Akbar household? Whatever the reason, it was doing wonders for her. Even during their brief conversation over the phone, she had seemed so much more ... Radha could not quite put her finger on it: Animated? Spirited? Free?

The car was encased in snow but in a way that was strangely pleasant, Radha noted for the first time that night. It felt more like a cocoon than a sarcophagus. She loosened the shawl around her shoulders, realizing that the car had generated enough heat while it was in motion to keep her warm now that it was stationary. The stillness and quiet made Radha mindful of her breathing in ways that generally eluded her, no matter how much the yogi had coached her. In and out, in and out, she watched her vaporous breath appear and disappear in the space before her. As her breathing grew steadier she became aware of how motionless she had been, frozen and dormant like the pine trees dotting the Akbars' lawn. But unlike the trees that worked hard to keep their roots strong and sturdy for the inevitable spring thaw, what had she been doing? What was she preparing for?

Radha looked out at the haze of lights outside the car. The snowstorm was easing up, moving eastward where it would meet the coastline and either lose steam and dissipate or gather even greater strength as it crossed the formidable Atlantic.

For a moment she could not remember why she was still in the car when the Akbars' house was only a few steps away. Focused, instead, on Mumtaz, who was likely anxious about dinner getting cold, she took another deep breath and exhaled. She hiked up her sari and slid over the central console, managing to manoeuvre herself into the driver's seat without ripping the silky material or getting it tangled up around the gear stick. Just as she reached for the lock on the driver's side, she heard a whirring sound, like a fan, emanating from outside the car.

"Don't worry, Radha! You'll be free in an instant!" she could hear Tariq call out to her from the passenger's side of the car.

The whirring continued and she could vaguely see Tariq holding some contraption up to the door handle. It was attached to a long cord that trailed all the way from the open garage, which now sent a clear beam of light down the length of the driveway. Later that night she would learn that the hair dryer was Mumtaz's idea; apparently, she had seen a neighbour perform this bizarre operation on more than one occasion. Of course, Tariq had taken full credit for it up until that point, joking that he was ready to resort to "whatever measures" the situation required, since he could well imagine Krishna suing him for damages should any harm come to his beloved wife or his equally precious "ten-thousand dollar door," on *his* property.

As foolish as Tariq felt about standing out in a snowstorm with a hair dryer, he was happy to come to Radha's rescue at Krishna's expense. Anything to bring him down a few pegs, he sneered. If it weren't for Mumtaz getting on his nerves about the invitation, asking who else they could count among their friends in this country, he would never have agreed to the dinner. After all, when was the last time *they* had received an invitation? He knew from the grapevine that their social life was busier than ever, and surely Krishna was well aware that Tariq could have benefited from an introduction to some of his new business contacts. For this reason alone, he had begrudgingly conceded to the dinner, concluding that if Krishna had gone up in the world, then he might as well keep that door open and use it to his advantage.

"Open Sesame!" Tariq said smugly, turning off the hair dryer and cranking open the door.

"Radha, what on earth are you doing there?" Krishna bellowed upon seeing his wife in the driver's seat.

"Well, it seems your wife managed to cross over, after all!" Tariq piped in, disgruntled for being imposed upon for nothing.

"If you had just bothered to ask me if I was all right *before* you turned on the hair dryer, I could have told you I had crossed over!"

"So why didn't you come out from the driver's side to save Tariq the trouble?"

"Because you both took so long to come out here that *this* door is frozen now!"

"Oh, that's it! We're going home!"

"Come, come, Krishna, it's no trouble at all. We wouldn't want Radha to cross over again, now would we?" Tariq mollified, remembering why he never cared much for Radha. He would never permit Mumtaz to talk to him like that. As pompous as Krishna was, he sympathized with any man who had to tolerate such an impious wife.

In a few minutes, Tariq thawed out the driver's side and

chivalrously offered his hand to the waiting damsel in distress.

Radha wrapped the shawl tightly around her shoulders, a gesture that prevented her from taking Tariq's hand. She ignored her husband's grimace, hiked up the sari *pallu* to prevent it from getting wet, and walked sure-footed across the snow-covered driveway to the Akbars' front door, where Mumtaz stood waiting with a piping hot mug of freshly brewed *chai*.

# OUTSIDE PEOPLE

"Tracy jumping Meena bed, Tracy breaking Meena head!" the new one we call Cat-Face shout. She call Cat-Face because she eyes green like real-life cat. Miss Benedict say there is cat so black only he green-green eyes make we know he really there.

"And you know what happen to them who go in the bush at night where the cat live?" Miss Benedict stop gathering the dirty sheet and place she-self on the edge of Meena bed.

Tracy stop jumping and we crowd round Miss Benedict. "Whathappen? Whathappen?"

"They never come back out the same way they go in," Miss Benedict say, looking deep into we eyes.

"Why?" I ask, grabbing Tracy hand because I know a "*nansi* story" coming.

"Because you can't see your shadow in the bush at night. You think you can, but is only the light of the moon playing tricks on you. Is only the branch of a jacaranda waving in the wind, or a spider monkey walking above you through the tall-tall trees. But the big black cat—the jaguar—is a special kind of animal. He see everything with eyes like magic lights that switch on in the dark. And he see what you can't see."

"What you can't see! What you can't see!" Tracy parrot Miss Benedict.

"If you cross the jaguar in the night…" Miss Benedict raise one of them sheet she gather and throw it on Tracy head.

"Look out! He steal your shadow before you even know you had one!" All ah we scream so loud we pee with laugh.

Miss Armstrong get up to go but I follow her. "Why we have to see we shadow, Miss Benedict?"

"Oh, Constance girl, you make me tired with all your questions. Your shadow is part of you, of course. How you know you really there if you can't see your shadow? If your shadow there beside you, you never alone. Is important to know you not the only little thing in this world." Since Miss Benedict tell we about the bush-cat what no one can see, Tracy stop jumping on Meena bed and start jumping on she shadow, saying the jaguar going to steal it.

"Lord have mercy! How many times I got to tell the Ministry about visiting hours! They think they can send anyone anytime," I hear House Mother voice like loud-speaker outside we room. Miss Benedict roll up the sheet and shuffle she big self into the next room where all them baby lie.

"Why they don't send some help instead, eh? Why they don't let them pickney kin take them home? How many times Meena grandma come round looking to take that child but the paper work not done? How many times Ministry say they not ready to release her? How many times I tell them about the others who get no visit since they been here—neither from they father nor they mother nor auntie nor uncle. Miss Tousignant and company sitting nice and comfy in them air-conditioned office sipping Coca Cola, while we is here sweating with more pickney coming every day. And still no help. Even Devon up and leave. *'I rather beat clothes by the trench than chase after them little devils!'* That what she say to me before she go!"

"Clothes-washing work don't sound so bad to me neither sometimes," Miss Benedict say all quiet-quiet.

"What you say?" House Mother mutter, while she hurrying to put some kind of bouncy spider thing over one of them baby bed. A little bell tinkle and I hear the baby make the happy noise, like he eat soap and bubble popping out of he mouth. House Mother smile too, giving the baby belly an extra rub so he make that happy noise again.

"Mrs. Armstrong!" I hear Paper Man call from the paper-room.

"Lord, them people here already!" House Mother say with a sigh so big it like hurricane pass through we rooms.

I can see the Outside People in the main hall. A man tall and thin like coconut tree stop to put down a big bag. The bag have a sticker on it with two red stripe and one white stripe and some kind of pointy red flower in the white stripe. It not like any flower I see before.

Paper Man come into the hall. "Mrs. Armstrong, please take these visitors to the girls," he call to House Mother again. "And don't forget to take the donations."

"Well, it was nice meeting you. And thanks for letting us in to see the girls on such short notice. We've travelled a long way...." I see Outside Lady shaking Paper Man hand.

"Yes, yes," Paper Man say. I can tell he making big-big effort to sound nice, but that only make him sound more impatient. "Here's Mrs. Armstrong. She'll show you around. And remember that it's very overwhelming at first."

O-wail-men. I try to repeat the word but it too hard for me tongue. Paper Man use too many big word I don't understand. So many big word Paper Man know, but he still don't know we name. He never say hello neither. He never ask how we is. Even House Mother and Miss Benedict always nicer when Paper Man not around. And they say all kind of funny thing about him that don't sound too good neither, though it take me a long time to understand that the man they calling Abdul is Paper Man. Once I hear Miss Benedict talk about Paper Man after he leave for the day: "What *her-highness* Mrs. Deoguardi think she doing sending that Abdul to us? He don't even know how many mouths we got to feed here! Why she don't hire a real manager to run this place proper?"

House Mother suck she teeth the way she do before she get vex with we. "How long I been telling Mrs. Deoguardi I been hired to run the school downstairs? How long that blackboard and chalk gathering dust and them desks fill-up with spiders? I got training to teach, you know, and all-of-it wasted on cleaning babies' bottoms and spending the live-long day tracking down this person to come fry plantain or that person to scrub them toilets. And what going to become of them girls running wild like so?"

Then Miss Benedict say, "Not just school-time cut since Abdul come. He cut out we staff too. First we lose Elsa. Then Devon. If they not fired they quit because they can't take it no more. And what this Abdul can do that nice volunteer girl Miss Aimsley can't do! Stupps! She better than Deoguardi and Abdul and all them Ministry people put together! At least she manage to get some babies out. At least she push Miss Tousignant to open she precious filing cabinet and look into things. At least she clean up the place good."

"What rubbish you talking, Leona? That Aimsley-girl worse than Abdul!" House Mother raise she voice and then, after looking over she shoulder into the main hall, she lower it again. "I rather have Abdul. At least I know what he about and he know to keep out of we business. At least he don't waltz in here for a day, turn we whole world upside-down and waltz back out, leaving we to put it all back together again. Them outsiders think they know everything, but what they know about life here, eh? What they know? The money we get to feed fifty children in one month they spend on one meal in fancy hotel. What they know about life in this place, eh?" House Mother start wiping one of the tables in the baby room hard-hard. Then she start up again: "And what about the mess Aimsley make before she go? I never seen Miss Tousignant so irate! Now the Ministry don't even send their officers here to check up on things no more. Okay, Aimsley get one-two child out while she here, but how many times

Mrs. Deoguardi blame *we* because that girl gone and done something she not authorized to do? Like that day she send Tracy to St. Mary's without knowing is a private hospital and the child get send back by taxi that *I* had to pay for from *me own* pocket! And then what she do? She take Tracy *back* to the hospital she *own-high-and-mighty-self* and make all kind of threat that if they don't treat the child she going to shame the Director in foreign newspaper."

"But Tracy could have died. Miss Aimsley save she life!" Miss Benedict say.

"I not saying I not happy the child get attention. I just saying what good it do for the rest of them? What we got to show for it now? We been banished from St. Mary's forever. At least before Aimsley cause all that botheration they would send one of them doctors every few months for check-up and what-not as part of they charity work. But when the last time Dr. Romano come round?" House Mother stop and point the dirty cloth she using to clean the table at Miss Benedict. "Better Abdul than Aimsley! Better we take care of we own."

"But Abdul take care of no one but he *own*-self. And he take all the credit when Mrs. Deoguardi and them Ministry people come. Like he own the place. Like he own all ah we and have to make we feel small-small when them big-shot sniffing 'round."

"Abdul not perfect," House Mother straighten she-self up and look into the main hall. "But every rope got two ends. I just saying he got bigger problem than this place. Even change his name when he come back."

"You mean his name not Abdul?"

"No girl! He look like he born a' Abdul' to you? His real name is Cartwright. He change it after he come out of hiding from the bush."

"What he hiding from?" Miss Benedict eyes turn big and round.

"He run away from that gold mining project in the interior.

He don't like what he see there. Nor what he had to do for the army."

"What he have to do for the army?"

"Ah, child, you more innocent than all them babies! What you think happen when Outside money get invested here and the army part of the deal? Cartwright, I mean Abdul, say things get real bad up there. Amerindians been living on that land long, long before all ah we get here. Sitting on mountains and rivers of gold, they say. Abdul say women and children getting the worst of it. His own *superior* take one of them girls for he own pleasure. And that not even the half of it! Abdul see the company dumping all kind of poison into the rivers."

"Why they need poison to get gold?"

"I look like scientist, child? What I know about these things! I just know the rivers getting poisoned and children being born with all kind of problem." House Mother turn to look at the baby we call Paw-Paw because she head shape all funny. And she not like them other baby that make me ears fill-up with they tears. Paw-Paw never make no sound.

"You mean Clara one of them?" Miss Benedict look at Paw-Paw too, then at House Mother, then at Paw-Paw again.

House Mother say nothing and she and Miss Benedict go back to whatever work they doing till I hear Miss Benedict ask, "So why Abdul change his name? They is after him or what?"

"Why else! After he run from the mining project he hide out with them Amerindians who run deep into the bush when they get chase out from they land. He say he go mad up there. He don't know how they get on surviving—some days without water, some days without light, some days with nothing to eat but cassava bread. He say he don't want to swallow another morsel of cassava if *Allah* bless it himself!" House Mother and Miss Benedict chuckle.

Then House Mother continue: "Finally he and some Amerindian boy escape on the boat that go up there once every month to give the army they supplies. The boy have a piece of gold, Abdul say—not even big enough to make wedding band but enough to pay the boatman to smuggle them back here. And once them make it back the boy just disappear. Abdul don't have nowhere to go neither till an old neighbour spot him at the market. That is how he find his way to the mosque. They treat him good, he tell me, like he their long-lost brother. He come to the faith on his own terms, he say, and then he come out of hiding. Don't ask me how he end up here, but is a real good thing he did. No one think to look for him here. They not supposed to have no political allegiance, you know. Maybe they give him protection if someone come looking."

"You mean Mrs. Deoguardi? Who she ever protected but she own kind?"

"This place much bigger than Mrs. Deoguardi! She just like to make we think she still queen of the castle. But this place only standing because of Outside money."

"So Abdul run from one Outside organization to another?"

"What can I say. Nothing make much sense in a place where the water never run clear."

"Mrs. Armstrong will show you where the babies are," I hear Paper Man say.

House Mother straighten she-self up and make the spider-thing stop bouncing up and down. Then she tell Outside People to come in. "They sleeping now so it best we leave them be," she say, though she not trying too hard to keep she voice down.

"We can't hold them?" Outside Lady ask.

I can see them better now. She have long gold hair like the doll no one play with no more. Tracy, Becca and Cat-Face pull on it so hard the arm-leg-head come right off. Cat-Face wail because she only come away with the doll arm, and Becca come away with the boobies part, but Tracy get the head and she comb the doll hair till it fall out from all them little holes. No one try to patch it up or play with it after that.

House Mother scrunch up she face and sing the little song

she sing whenever Outside People come: "Well-if-you-pick-one-up-you-have-to-pick-all-them-up-and-if-you-wake-them-now-they-won't-sleep-through-the-night-and-if-you-hold-one-now-they-cry-and-cry-till-they-held-again-and-the-good-Lord-only-give-we-two-arms-to-hold-his-treasures."

"Of course, I don't want to upset the children or their routine. I can't imagine how difficult it must be for you," Outside Lady say.

The lady have a nice voice and she smile a lot when she talk. Most of them Outside People don't smile. They just make face like Becca make when she have to eat soursop. But Outside Lady lose she smile when she see Paw-Paw. When Mrs. Armstrong see Outside Lady going to Paw-Paw, she look like she about to say something but she turn and leave the room even though Paper Man tell she to stay with Outside People.

"What race and age you looking for?" Miss Benedict say.

Outside Lady turn away from Paw-Paw. "Oh dear, we haven't really thought about that, but we've been approved for an infant. Zero to twenty-four months. We can't have a child of our own, you see."

"Boy or girl?"

"Either," Outside Man answer this time. He place one hand on Outside Lady back while she look into the bed where House Mother put the spider thing: "Look how cute this one is! He's so small. He can't be more than six months old."

"Oh, not Mrs. Armstrong boy—" Miss Benedict start to say and then bite she lip hard-hard, same like when we know we done something what can never be undone.

"You mean she's going to adopt him?" Outside Lady ask, pulling the spider-thing and making it tinkle again.

"No, I mean ... that one been here almost since the day he born. It hard not to think of them as we own. Besides, none of them babies ready for adoption."

"And why is that?" Outside Man ask.

"Because we don't know if they mother or father be coming back for them."

"You mean to say the children aren't abandoned? Then why are they here?" Outside Lady ask.

"Sometimes they parents just got nowhere else to leave them. Sometimes they come back for them; sometimes they don't. Like Constance, our oldest."

Miss Benedict talking about me! I turn to push Tracy and Meena away but they already bored by the Outside People and move far from the gate that separate we room from the baby room.

"Constance been here too-too many years—so we call her we oldest." Miss Benedict stop to look over she shoulder. Outside People facing Miss Benedict, but they eyes look like they searching for someone and no one at the same time.

"People been flying to your country like bees to a honey pot for a long time now," Miss Benedict continue. "There are probably more of us up there then there are down here! I got family there too, you know—in Toronto. Is that where you from?"

"Ottawa," Outside Man say.

"I hear all about Ottawa from my cousin Samuel. He say it get so cold there the river freeze up every year and become a big long road and playground all winter long."

"It's a canal," Outside Man correct Miss Benedict.

Miss Benedict don't seem to notice. "Well, Constance mother is one of them bees. But she only get visa for she-self, not for she daughter. The day she leave, she take Constance to the airport and tell she child to wait where them sell sweets and things. The poor thing just stand there for two-three hours before the man at the counter ask what she doing there—not because he care but because he think the child making ready to steal something. That how Constance remember it ... what she tell the police when the man call them to take she away."

"You mean her mother left her at the airport? How cruel!"

Outside Lady say, wiping something from she eye.

"She been waiting for she mama to come back ever since."

"This is outrageous! Surely the State can assume legal guardianship of an abandoned child! Why in God's name hasn't she been adopted or fostered, at the very least?" Outside Man say, using big word and looking impatient like Paper Man.

"People don't get too much help for that sort of thing here. If the child got family, the family usually take them. But is much more complicated when plenty family live outside. And not many people willing to feed another mouth when they got so little to survive on. Still, as hard as things are now is not like before when Constance mother leave. Those were some real bad days. People standing in line for bread, for rice, for soap, any little thing they could get, and too-too much trouble because nobody know if it's freedom from 'outside' we get or freedom from 'inside' we need. With half we people living up there where you come from—living everywhere but here—the Ministry trying hard to stop the country from losing more of its own, trying hard to keep we pickney down here...." Miss Benedict not able to finish her thought because House Mother come back and say something to Outside People.

"Oh no! We were hoping to spend some time with the girls! And give them some of the toys..." Outside Lady say. She try to smile again, but she face look like Meena face the day the small-small woman leave her with us without saying so much as a good afternoon. It raining hard-hard that day and the woman float into the house with a river of water dripping from she clothes and hair. When House Mother put Meena in we room, we couldn't tell if she wet from the rain or wet from she tears. Like someone rip open she sky.

"Maybe another day," I hear House Mother again. "The Ministry not supposed to treat we like some open house ... I mean send visitors so close to suppertime, after the babies settle down for the night."

Outside People not come back the next day nor the next day

after that. Tracy laugh and say the jaguar steal they shadow. She say same thing happen to Mama too.

What Tracy know about that? What she know about Miss Benedict stories?

# GLOSSARY

**AIR RAIDS**
(French words and phrases)

*Métro* — the subway system in the city of Montreal
*dépanneur* — corner store or convenience store
VIVE LE QUÉBEC LIBRE POUR TOUS — long live Quebec for everyone
*Qu'est-ce que tu t'en souviens de notre première rencontre?* — What do you remember of our first encounter?
*Que nous avons oublié nos destinations. Tu as manqué ton arrêt, et moi, le mien* — That we forgot where we were going. You missed your stop and I missed mine.
*Et quand tu as vu ce pendentif tu as pensé que je suis, comme toi, Arabe* — And when you saw this pendant, you thought I am, like you, an Arab.
*Donc, nous sommes d'une seule famille* — Then we are part of the same family.
*beau corps* — beautiful body
*tu fumes trop* — you smoke too much
*peut-être* — maybe, perhaps
*rien* — nothing
LA DIVERSITÉ EST UNE RICHESSE — diversity is a resource
ÉTAT LAÏC, INDIVIDUS LIBRES — secular state, free individuals
QUÉBEC JE ME SOUVIENS — Québec, I remember
*comme tu peux voir* — as you can see

*Alors, c'est possible de me retrouver aussi* — then it is possible to find me too

**(Arabic words and phrases)**
*surah* — a chapter from the Quran; a Quranic verse
*ayat al-kursi* — The Verse of the Throne (Surah 2-255), in the Holy Quran
*iftar* — the communal meal served at sunset during the month of Ramadan
*hijab* — (literally, 'cover' in Arabic) headscarf or head covering worn by some Muslim women
*halal* — (literally, 'lawful' or 'permitted') foods deemed permissible for consumption under Islamic law; or the dietary set of guidelines practiced by Muslims
*niqab* — a face covering the mouth and nose worn by some Muslim women
*Wahabi* — a member of the religious movement or sect founded by Muhammad ibn Abd Al-Wahhab in the eighteenth century, and the official state-sanctioned form of Sunni Islam practiced by the vast majority in Saudi Arabia

**(Urdu words and phrases)**
*Shalwar kameez* — traditional outfit worn by women in South Asia, consisting of long loose pants, a knee length or hip-length "kameez" or tunic, and a dupatta (long scarf)

CHICKEN CATCHERS
**(Spanish words and phrases)**

*Ándale, amigo!* — let's go, friend!
*No solamente un pollo por mano, hermanito! Cuatro pollos por mano!* — not just one chicken per hand, brother! Four chickens per hand!
*Hasta luego!* — see you later!

*Comprendes?* — do you understand?
*Vámanos!* — Let's go (imperative)
*esperame!* — wait for me (imperative)
*muy cansado* — very tired
*todo el tiempo* — all the time
*cómo se dice* — how do you say it?
*Digame* — tell me (imperative)
*dinero* — money
*Discúlpame* — excuse me; forgive me
*Como la ciudad* — like the city
*Aqui, muy extraños* — here, very strange
*Lo más sabroso* — the tastiest
*mi hija* — my daughter
*el patrón* — the boss
*no puedo!* — I cannot!


(Jamaican Creole words and phrases)
*callalloo* — a popular Caribbean soup of mixed leafy greens originating in West Africa
*cha!* — expression of disapproval, frustration
*me cyaan lef yuh deh* — I can't leave you like that
*nuh jus one way fi heng dog* — there's more than one way to get things done/achieve a goal
*naah mean* — you know what I mean (Jamaican slang)
*bredda* — brother
*bakra* — the white slave-master


CORAZON'S CHILDREN
(Tagalog words and phrases)

*Maganda* — beautiful
*hindi-po* — no (formal)
*salamat-po* — thank you (formal)

# GLOSSARY

*Mahal kita* — I love you


## Toronto's Dominions
(Hindi/Urdu words and phrases)

*abbu-ji* — term of endearment for father (using the affectionate suffix 'ji')
*hungama* — quarrel or commotion
*beti* — term of endearment for daughter
*haldi* — turmeric
*Chana masala* — (literally chick peas and mixed spices) a popular Indian/Pakistani vegetarian dish consisting primarily of chick peas
*Vindaloo* — originally a Goan meat dish popularized in Indian restaurants in the West
*naan* — traditional baked flat bread in North Indian and Pakistani cuisine
*khana* — food
*haramzada* — a jerk
*mandap* — the altar or dais where Hindus perform their wedding rites
Patak's — a popular British-Indian brand of chutney, pickles and South Asian curry pastes


## SUNSHINE GUARANTEE
(Spanish words and phrases)

*Dios mio* — my God
*Siete Mares* — seven seas
*no hay lluvia* — there is no rain
*no seas tonta* — don't be silly
*mira* — look
*pueblos* — towns

*la iglesia* — church
*la misa* — mass
*dulces de guayaba* — confectionary made from the guava fruit
*plátanos fritos* — fried plantains
*enamorada con la muerte* — enamoured with death
*pórtate bien cuatito, si no te lleva el coloradito* — behave yourself my friend, or the devil will take you (pithy proverb used in the Mexican lottery)
*con respeto* — with respect; respectfully
*por dios!* — goodness! (oh God!)
*papas fritas* — French fries
*quetzal* — a tropical bird native to Meso-America
*Madrecita* — mother (using affectionate diminutive suffix 'ita')
*pendejo* — idiot; jerk
*Que fufurufo es* — what a show-off he is
*Los pueblos originales* — native peoples
*La brujería* — witchery
*gringos* — foreigners
*turistas* — tourists
*dime* — tell me (imperative)
*hijo* — son
*nuevo mundo* — new world
*abuelita* — grandmother (using affectionate diminutive suffix 'ita')
*El Papa* — The Pope
*tamarindo* — tamarind fruit
*Sopas* — a colloquial expression of frustration
*Casados* — married
*negritas* — colloquial racialized term for women of African origin
*telenovela* — generic term for Latin American soap operas
*Inglaterra* — England
*Sudamérica* — South America
*Explícame* — explain it to me (imperative)
*campesinos* —peasants

*esclavos* — slaves
*mestizaje* — mixed race
*la mariposa monarca* — monarch butterfly
*babosa* — airhead
*Créeme* — believe me (imperative)
*Sol, solo te quedaste, de cobija de los pobres* — alone, only you remain to protect the poor (pithy proverb used in the Mexican lottery)

## BREAD AND ROTI
(Urdu words and phrases)

*roti* — a generic term for bread
*Ammi* — Mother
*maulana* — a scholar of Islam
*bhai* — brother (also used colloquially for males, as a show of affection or respect)
*khuda ke fazal* — by God's grace
*masjid* — mosque
*sahiba* — Ma'am or Mrs. (female equivalent to "Sahib" for Mister or Sir)
*bibi* — lady/wife (used colloquially for females, as a show of respect)
*itni dur-dur* — so far
*bhain* — sister (also used colloquially for females, as a show of affection or respect)
*Bhookh laghe hai!* — we're hungry
*Mein bookha hun* — I'm hungry
*chapati* — a flat bread made on a hot cast-iron pan
*tawa* — a flat pan
*ghee* — clarified butter
*roti-makhan-chini* — bread-butter-sugar (part of a child's nursery rhyme)
*gora* — white person

*karó* (channel change *karó*) — an imperative of the verb to do
*haram* — something that is prohibited under Islamic law
*gunha* — sin
*Bicahri* — poor thing
*Ammi, sab kuch samji* — did you get that (understand everything)
*Wo parinda kahan gaya hai* — where did the bird go
*mithai* — sweetmeats usually made from sweetened milk
*biryani* — elaborate rice and meat dish served on special occasions
*haleem* — a rich barley dish served on special occasions
*haji* — one who has completed "*haj*" or the pilgrimage to Mecca
*Imam* — prayer leader or the head of a mosque
*bachiyan* — children (female)
*izzat* — concept of honour, respect or reputation
*Acha—jaldi batao* — okay, tell me quickly
*Apka mian* — your husband
*gori ke sath* — with a white girl
*sath* — with
*manat* — a pledge, in Islam, to give charity as a show of gratitude for God's blessings
*lunghi* — a fabric wrap worn by males
*Ammi, mein bahar ja raha hun* — Mother, I'm going out
*Nahin jao* — don't go
*Fikur nahin* — don't worry
*shalwar kameez* — traditional outfit worn by women in South Asia, consisting of long loose pants, a knee length or hip-length "*kameez*" or tunic, and a *dupatta* (long scarf); the three pieces together are often referred to as a "suit"
*Bhookh laga hai, chota parinda? Bhookh laga hai?* — Are you hungry, little bird? Are you hungry?
*Mein ab sab-kuch samajti hun. Apka Abba ke pas jaraha hai* — I understand everything now. You are going to your father.
*Bhathiye!* — sit down (imperative/command form)
*Bilkul Abba ke jaysa hai* — He's just like his father

## THIRTY-FIVE SECONDS
(Haitian Kreyole)

*Bondye bon* —God is good
*Bondye beni ou*—God bless you
*Woch nan dlo pa konnen doulé wòch nan solèy* —The rock in the water does not know the pain of the rock in the sun
*Si mwen menm ki ta dwe mande padon* — it is I who should ask your forgiveness
*Bondye nou an Fidel* — God protects us; God will never give us up


## CROSSING OVER
(Hindi/Urdu words and phrases)

*As-Salam Alaikum* — (Arabic: peace be upon you) traditional Muslim greeting
*W'Alaikum Salam* — (Arabic: and unto you peace) the customary response to *as-salam alaikum*
*Namaste* — traditional Hindu greeting
*fanoos* — (Arabic: lamp or light); a traditional ornamental hanging lantern found in Morocco and Egypt
*chai* — a tea consumed across much of the Indian subcontinent, usually cooked with milk, sugar and a variety of spices
*ghee* — clarified butter
*bindi* — a Hindu custom of adorning a woman's forehead with a red dot, usually to indicate that she is married
*(sari) pallu* — the decorated border or hem of a *sari* (traditional women's attire worn across the Indian subcontinent)

# ACKNOWLEDGEMENTS

I am delighted to see this first collection published by Inanna, under the editorship of Luciana Ricciutelli. Profound thanks to you, Luciana, and your intrepid crew, for expertly navigating this tipsy craft to safe harbour.

I am fortunate to be surrounded by individuals whose creative energy, wit, and wisdom inspire at every turn; in this regard, I am especially grateful to my cherished and supremely accomplished comrades, Tanis MacDonald and Philippa Gates. Thanks also to Tamas Dobozy and Tanis MacDonald for proving that it is possible to conduct an academic and creative life in productive harmony. And thanks to Eleanor Ty for bringing "Corazon's Children" (in its earliest iteration) to the attention of her students, and to the rest of my dear colleagues of the Department of English and Film Studies at Wilfrid Laurier University for their uniquely patented brands of friendship and support.

Beyond university halls, Waterloo-based activist Ulises Fuentes is owed my sincere thanks for taking the time to share his insights regarding the plight of the migrant agricultural worker in Southern Ontario.

To my family, I owe everything. The enduring love and unflinching support of my father, Rafiq Pirbhai, is always near at hand, as is the special kind of passport to the world that has been and continues to be his self-replenishing gift to me. And every story I tell is animated by the irrepressible creativity and quiet resilience of my late mother, Qamar Iqbal.

I am awed, as always, by my brother Reza Pirbhai, for his fierce intelligence, effortless artistry and enviable command of Urdu (!), and my sister Nooreen Pirbhai, for a depth of conviction that is equally matched by her depth of compassion: thank you both for giving me a kinship, a friendship, and a source of emotional and intellectual nourishment that is as invaluable as air. I am blessed to be part of our very special little family of global misfits, including your beautiful life partners and children: Reem Meshal and Ilyas; Mandeep Flora and Zahya. (And a very special note of thanks is due to Mandeep, for opening a door to a vital segment of the South Asian Canadian diaspora, allowing me to deepen my connections therein.)

To my husband, Ronaldo Garcia, who lives with my stories as intimately as I do, be it as beloved muse, cultural conduit, keen translator, patient sounding board, or adoring partner: these words take flight with you and find meaning through you, always.

# NOTES

The story "Outside People" was first published in *Maple Tree Literary Supplement,* Issue # 19 (May-August 2015). It was also re-printed in a backdated special creative issue, edited by Ameena Gafoor, of *The Arts Journal* (TAJ), Vol 10.1 & 2 (2014-2015): 14-20.

An earlier version of "Air Raids" was first published in the anthology *Her Mother's Ashes III: Stories by South Asian Women in Canada and the United State*s, edited by Nurjehan Aziz (Toronto: TSAR, 2009: 114-123). Print.

An earlier version of "Sunshine Guarantee," was first published in a special creative issue titled "Pakistani Creative Writing in English (Tracing the Tradition: Embracing the Emerging)," guest edited by Waseem Anwar and Fawzia Afzal-Khan, of the *South Asian Review* Vol. 31.3 (2010): 274-288.

The epigraphs appear with permission from Sheep Meadow Press and The Monthly Press.

Note also that the poetic stanza in "Crossing Over" is extracted from the poem "Prometheus" by Lord (George Gordon) Byron (1816).

Photo: John Ternan

Mariam Pirbhai was born in Pakistan, and lived in England and the Philippines before emigrating to Canada. She lives in Waterloo, Ontario, where she is an Associate Professor in the Department of English and Film Studies, at Wilfrid Laurier University. She has published several academic books in the field of postcolonial and diaspora studies. Her short stories have appeared in numerous anthologies and literary journals, in Canada and abroad. *Outside People and Other Stories* is her debut collection of short fiction.